LUCY PEALE

COLBY RODOWSKY

Lucy

Peale

FARRAR, STRAUS AND GIROUX

NEW YORK

For some special friends in the
Washington Children's Book Guild:
Rebecca Jones, Phyllis Naylor, Mary Claire Helldorfer,
and Gene Namovicz

LUCY PEALE

One

"Can I have it?" said Liddy, her voice sounding muffled as she crawled backward out of the closet.

"Have what? And be quiet besides. It's early yet," said Lucy. She tugged at the pillow and felt it damp against her face. She opened her eyes to the hard morning sunlight, then closed them again. The heat in the room pushed down around her, making her body feel heavy. Her mouth had a sweet-and-sour taste and she swallowed carefully to keep her stomach from rising up against it.

"Can I?" said Liddy.

"Whatever it is, no. And leave me be," said Lucy.

"I'm gonna tell," said Liddy.

"Praise the Lord," squawked their mother's parrot from the floor below.

3

"Shut that fool bird up," said Lucy. She turned carefully to face the wall, pulling the torn sheet over her head.

"You shouldn't ought to talk that way," said Liddy. "Pa'll skin you alive. You know what he says the Bible says about calling one's kinfolk a fool and then forever after burning up in hell. Something like that."

" 'He who calls his brother a fool shall burn in the fires of hell' is what he says and that bird's not my brother and it *is* a fool and it's dumb besides and can't hardly say anything and it doesn't even have a name," said Lucy, feeling suddenly wide awake and hotter than she had before, but still keeping the sheet pulled up over her head.

"That shows what *you* know, Lucy *pill* Peale. 'Praise the Lord' *is* its name and when it says that it's just saying who it is, same as if I said Liddy and you said Lucy and Doris said Doris and Warren said Warren and Ma said Ma and Pa said—"

"And I for one devoutly wish it'd *shut up*—and you along with it."

"Shouldn't ought to say 'shut up' either. Pa'll make you repent. 'Fool' and 'shut up' all in one day. He'll make you stand up there in the service and say out loud what you already said."

"Won't neither," said Lucy. She opened her eyes and watched the light filter through the sheet, then closed them again.

"Praise the Lord," shouted the bird.

"Can I *have* it?" said Liddy, sitting cross-legged on the floor next to her sister's bed.

"Have what?"

"The dog."

4

"What dog? We don't have any dog."

"The dog I found," said Liddy. "That's what I've been asking you—can I have it."

"Pa'd never let you," said Lucy. "You know what he says about no pets nohow. 'Cept for that stupid bird."

"Not a *real* dog, but *yours.* Can I *have* it?" whined Liddy.

"I don't have a dog. Except . . ." Lucy sat up suddenly, pressing her back flat against the wall and staring down at her little sister, who held a stuffed white dog with long floppy ears and red letters saying *Ocean City, Maryland* emblazoned along its side. "Where'd you get that?"

"Out of the closet. I told you I found it, didn't I," said Liddy.

"What were you doing in my closet?" said Lucy.

"It's mine too, same as yours. Mine and Doris's. And I was in *my* part of *my* closet looking for something and I saw this here white fuzzy thing stuffed up under the rafters and I pulled it out and it was this dog with its fur all dustied up from where the ceiling meets the wall. And"— she went on, licking her lips—"I'll tell Pa and he'll want to know where you got it from—unless I can *have* it."

"Put it back," said Lucy, pushing herself into a standing position and lurching sideways as her feet sank into the mattress. "Put it back. It's nasty and rotten and spoiled and I don't want to see it ever again."

"I'll clean it, then," said Liddy, spitting on the ends of her fingers and rubbing at a smudge of dirt over the dog's left ear. "And I'll keep it in a berry basket under my bed, like it was a real live dog, and Pa'll never see it and never have to know how you came to get something from Ocean City when the onliest time any of us've ever been there is when he took us himself so's we could hand out flyers on the boardwalk for the tent service."

"Give me that dog," said Lucy, swallowing hard and feeling the room tilt around her. "Give it to me."

"I'm gonna tell, then," said Liddy. She slid back across the floor and stood up, holding the toy dog on top of her head so that its floppy legs dangled on either side of her face like fat white curls. "How you've got something you're not meant to have and how you and Doris've likely been sneaking over across the bridge and into town at night. Into *Sin* City, like Pa calls it."

"It's Ocean City, and we never did," said Lucy. "Somebody gave it to me, is all. But it's dirty and I want it away from here." She watched for a minute as her sister pranced around the room, wearing the dog like a wig. Then she lunged, grabbing it by the tail and holding it at arm's length as she ran out into the hall, down the steps, and through the screen door at the bottom, pushing it so hard that it flew open and hung there, flat against the wall. She heard Liddy behind her and ran faster, cutting across the grass and onto the rutted dirt road between the house and the tent. Her hair whipped against her face and she felt her nightgown clinging to her body, the stones and stubble digging into her bare feet. She pushed her way through the underbrush and onto the narrow beach at the edge of the bay and out into the water till it lapped around her knees. Then she swung back and hurled the dog as far as she could. Liddy came up beside her and together they watched as the stuffed animal bobbed there for a minute before it grew heavy with water and finally sank.

Liddy howled and Lucy cried out, "Good—I'm glad it's

gone from here." Suddenly her legs shook and she felt tears running down her face. Her mouth filled with saliva, her stomach lurched, and she turned and slogged back through the water and across the beach to the side of a wooden shed, where, holding on to one weathered wall, she vomited into a patch of poison ivy. Afterwards she stood leaning against the wall with her arms locked across her stomach. Her nose burned and her eyes stung as she took a long quivering breath, spit, and rubbed at her mouth with the back of her hand.

Behind her she heard Liddy turn and start for the house, calling as she ran, "Ma, Lucy's throwing up down by the shed same as she throws up every morning 'cept she thinks nobody knows but I *hear* her and it's disgusting. And besides she had this dog that said *Ocean City, Maryland* on the side and she shouldn't ought to've had it 'cept she did but now she's gone and thrown it in the bay and I *wanted* it."

Lucy waited until her sister disappeared around the side of the house before she made her way back to the beach, where she fell in a heap on the sand and lay curled on her side with her head on her arms. She tried to concentrate on the sound of the water as it washed up onto the shore and to keep her mind free of the thoughts that pushed against it: thoughts of the stuffed dog, lost now somewhere in the muck at the bottom of the bay; of the boy who had given it to her and the smell of him in the car that night. She tried not to think of the sickness that had taken hold of her the last few weeks, even as she balled her hand into a fist and pressed it hard against her stomach.

After a while she stood up and went back through the

underbrush and along the road, stopping by the side of the tent and leaning on the sign that said *Church of the Saving Grace* in lopsided red letters. She looked at the sky overhead, bleached white as bone, and felt the silence that crowded around her. She darted across the road, staying close to the house and ducking down as she passed the windows and made her way around to the front. She stopped for a minute, holding her breath and listening, before she stepped onto the porch and pulled open the screen door.

They were waiting inside, the five of them, drawn back into the corner, away from the splotch of sunlight that spilled from the open door onto the linoleum. Lucy saw them there like an old photograph with the color washed away: her father in his dark trousers, his dingy white shirt and scraggly tie, his eyes tucked back in his round moon face; her mother, thin and pale and wispy, with her hair hanging lank, her socks creeping down her heels and into her shoes; her sister Doris, at eighteen a year older than Lucy, and Warren, the youngest, poised on one foot, pulled back toward the rest as if by an invisible leash. And, off to the side, there was Liddy, looking wide-eyed and uncertain at what she had brought about.

After what seemed like hours her father spoke, his voice loud and piercing, as if he were filling all the reaches of the tent and not just that small hot room.

"Clothe your nakedness, Lucy Peale. Clothe your nakedness."

Lucy looked down, smoothing the crinkled cotton nightgown, then crossing her arms across her chest. "I am clothed, Pa. And, besides, I've got my underpants on underneath."

"Don't sass me," he said.

And before Lucy could answer that she wasn't sassing, that she was speaking the truth, he picked up a quilt off the end of the couch and threw it at her. The quilt was thin and faded from too many washings and smelled slightly musty. It was made up of squares, one for each book of the Bible, and Lucy pulled it close around her, holding tight to Exodus and Leviticus and feeling the lumpy stitches her mother had made many years ago.

Edgar Peale cleared his throat, and when he spoke this time his voice was low and hard, so that Lucy had to lean forward to hear him. "What do you have to say, Lucy Peale?" he asked.

"Nothing *to* say," said Lucy.

"Nothing? Nothing?" Now her father's voice grew and swelled and pounded down against her. "Nothing to say about what your sister tells me about running off into town, about some gimcrack smuggled in from the outside. About the sickness every morning—as if I didn't know the meaning of *that*."

"I never did—run off into town, I mean—and about the rest, I don't know," said Lucy, and though the room was hot and her hair stuck to the back of her neck, she shivered and pulled the quilt tighter around her.

"Well, *I* know," said her father. "I know about Sodom and Gomorrah across the bay and about sending my children into town to preach the Word of the Lord. How I sent them there to hand out flyers to try and coax the sinners away from the lights and the music and the carryings-on, and back across the bridge so's they could give testament to the Lord here with Preacher Peale and the Church of the Saving Grace. I know how in the time after that somebody came and trampled up what belongs to me and mine.

"And do you know how I know? I'll tell you how I know. I'll tell you how I went out one morning early in the summer and found the trappings of sin—the beer cans and the whiskey bottles down on the road and the cigarette butts ground into the Lord's green grass. And how I cleaned it up myself and buried it deep in the ground just so's the rest of you would never need to know how somebody'd come in the night and polluted us all."

Lucy felt weak and suddenly drained as if it had taken all her strength to push against the memory of that night. She moved closer to her mother, but her mother turned from her, reaching out instead for Liddy and starting to braid the younger girl's hair.

"And you were a part of that pollution. Am I right?"

Lucy forced herself to stand there, not to fall under the weight of her father's words. Out of the corner of her eye she saw Doris start forward, saw her open her mouth as if to say that she had been there that night along with Lucy.

"Am I right, Lucy Peale?" thundered her father.

"I was there, Pa. Me by myself. Me and just some boys that came out from town, reading the directions on the flyer and following the signs. And this one boy, he gave me something—that toy stuffed dog with the writing on the side, the one that Liddy found—only I didn't want it and I hid it away."

"He gave you something else, too, didn't he?" said her

father, stepping close and jabbing at her with his short, stubby finger.

"I don't know, Pa. I don't remember," said Lucy.

"He gave you what's there in your belly. What's making you sick in the mornings.

"He gave you sin."

"My baby's no sin," cried Lucy, suddenly acknowledging the existence of the child that she hadn't admitted, even to herself, before. "My baby's no bad thing."

The room was quiet except for the sound of the parrot scratching at his cage on the table. Preacher Peale moved over to stand by the screen door, looking out. After a while he turned back into the room, poking his fingers into a pyramid and rocking forward on his toes. "As a mouse eats cheese from a trap, so are the fleeting pleasures of sin," he said.

"But we're going to take this sin and bust it wide open," he went on. "We're going to take this sin and make it some kind of blessing and we're going to watch as Lucy Peale comes forward at the service tonight and repents for all the world to see. And we're going to listen as Lucy Peale says, 'Thank you, Jesus, for giving me this sin and giving me a way to show that even a Jezebel can turn her life around.' Because if she doesn't, then she's no kin of mine any-more—and there's no place for her in this house.

"Isn't that right?" He turned to his wife, to Doris and Warren and Liddy, and waited until, one by one, they all nodded.

"Isn't that right, Lucy Peale?" he said.

Lucy stood without saying anything.

"Isn't that right?" her father asked again, stepping close to her and leaning forward so that she felt his breath against her face.

"Yes, Pa. Yes," said Lucy.

"Praise the Lord," called the parrot from his cage.

Two

The tent was hot. Lucy lifted her hair off her neck and fanned herself with her hand. She reached in her pocket and pulled out a Kleenex, wiping her face and the insides of her elbows. She pushed out her lower lip, blew, and felt the air on her cheeks, her nose, her eyes. She peeled her skirt away from the backs of her legs.

All around her, people swayed from side to side, their heads rolling back, their eyes closed. They moaned and writhed and threw their hands out in front, as if reaching for something, and shuffled their feet in the sawdust heaped there on the wooden floor. The woman next to her cried "Hallelujah" and Lucy moved closer to Doris, wishing she could disappear inside herself. Up on the platform, her father swung his tambourine overhead and called out, "How many love Jesus tonight?"

There was a muttering, a few scattered "I do"s.

"How many?" prodded the preacher. "How many?"

"I do—I do—I do—" The sound rose and rippled through the crowd.

"I don't hear you so good," he cried. "How many out there love Jesus?"

The voices swelled and filled the tent, bouncing off the sides and swirling around the center pole and up to the top.

"I do—I do . . ."

"Praise the Lord . . ."

"Amen."

Lucy saw her father grab for the microphone and hold it high before he brought it close to his mouth and called out, "If you love Him, then let's glorify Him tonight." She saw her mother crouched low over the little organ, pressing down on the keys and forcing out a thin, wheezy music. She watched as Warren moved onto the platform and beat his tambourine against the side of his leg, as Liddy took up a guitar almost as big as she was.

"Hallelujah, but I've got revival in my soul," her father half sang, half said. " 'Cause there've been times in this sweet life when I've been down, but when I'm down I know that Jesus hasn't forgot me." He was all over the platform, sweeping from one side to the other, rushing up close to the edge, then backing off. His face was red and shiny and his hair stood out around his head. He pulled off his suit coat and threw it down as he shouted, "Have you thought what it's like to be on the Lord's side, 'cause the Lord's side is the winning side and when you're on the winning side that's the time to be happy. Are you happy tonight?"

"That's right," came a voice from the crowd.

"Say it again," came another voice.

"Say it again," said the preacher, the microphone taking his words and turning them into a whistle.

"That's right," shouted the crowd. Lucy put her hands up to her ears. She caught her breath and stepped back, feeling the heat pulsing through the tent. She looked over to the side where the flaps were up and saw that the light had faded, that the sky was dark. "I got to get out of here," she whispered to Doris as her father reached for his Bible and held it up over the crowd. "Before Pa starts into his sermon." She pushed past the woman next to her and stepped over a little boy shaping mountains out of sawdust on the floor and made her way up the aisle between the chairs, with Doris close behind her.

"Where're you going?" said Doris when they were outside and had moved away from the flap.

"Noplace. Anyplace. To get some air so's I can breathe on account of it smells in there, like sweat and skin and tent canvas," said Lucy, swatting at a mosquito as it landed on her arm.

"They'll eat you alive out here," said Doris. "The mosquitoes, I mean."

"They'll eat me alive in *there*," said Lucy. "Besides, Pa said after the sermon is when I got to come forward and that gives me an hour, maybe more, if he really gets fired up."

"Yeah, but what if he sees you're not there now," said Doris.

"Maybe he won't," said Lucy. "Leastways, maybe he won't if you go back in there and he doesn't see a big empty

15

space where we're meant to be, if you sort of spread out and make like you're two people."

"I guess," said Doris, kicking at the dirt in the road. Finally she looked up at Lucy and said, "I just want you to know that all day I've felt real bad for not telling Pa how it was the two of us together on the night the boys came out from town. And this morning, when he said what he did about sin and there maybe not being anyplace for you in his house, a part of me wanted to stand up straight and look him in the eye and say that it was me *and* Lucy. Except I didn't. Except I couldn't." She stopped for a minute, pulling on a strand of hair before going on. "Same as tonight a part of me wants to get up there with you, to go forward after the sermon when Pa calls for the sinners, except—"

"No," said Lucy, looking at the fear in her sister's eyes. "No, it's nothing to do with you. It's me it happened to. It's me Pa caught. It's me now that'll do what he says— that'll stand when he says stand, and move to the front when he yells 'Repent.' It's me that'll do all these things on account of I don't know what else *to* do." Lucy bit down hard on her lip. Then she reached out for Doris and gave her a little shove. "You get on back now so's I can have some thinking time. Me by myself."

After Doris had gone, Lucy stood for a minute, listening to the sounds from inside the tent. She heard the rustle and clatter as everyone moved to sit down, heard her father's voice spilling out over the crowd as he started into his sermon. "Praise the name of the Lord," he began. She knew that by now he would be pacing back and forth on the platform, holding the Bible in one hand, the other clenched into a fist around the microphone.

"Preach on," called a voice from the congregation.

"Preach on."

"Preach on."

Lucy moved down the road away from the tent, making her way between cars parked up on the grass and crowded into the underbrush. She went until her father's voice grew blurred and indistinct, the words running into one another, then she stopped and stood leaning on a pickup truck. After a while she climbed up and sat on the hood, feeling the heat of the day still trapped in the metal, and looking across the bay toward town. The sky over Ocean City was aglow and Lucy closed her eyes, seeing again the lights that outlined the Ferris wheel, the merry-go-round, and all the other rides jumbled there at the end of the boardwalk. All of a sudden the wind changed and she caught the throb of music as it drifted over the water.

Right from the start I knew this place'd be different, thought Lucy, pulling her knees up under her chin and remembering how ever since they moved here she had liked to go out alone at night and watch the lights. Right from the start I knew it'd be different'n those other places Pa was always dragging us to, setting up his tent in some vacant field and putting his signs out along the highway. Moving us into some ratty-tatty house or broken-down trailer.

"Not that this place's so all-fired special," she said out loud, looking back at the house, its peeling paint leaving it gray and shiny in the moonlight. "Except for it's got Ocean City just across the way there.

"Ocean City, Ocean City, Ocean City," Lucy chanted under her breath.

Only Pa had called it Sin City from the very first, she thought. And said how it was the Devil's playground and how one day we'd go there and tell folks about the Church of the Saving Grace.

"And we did," said Lucy, as she brushed at a mosquito close to her ear and looked from the light in the sky across the bay to the light spilling out of the tent. She remembered the Friday night of the Memorial Day weekend when her father had pushed back from the supper table and said, "Get your Sunday clothes on now 'cause we're fixing to go into town and do the work of the Lord." She remembered crowding into the car with Pa and Doris, with Liddy and Warren, and heading down the back road to the highway and then onto the bridge.

Lucy caught her breath, the way she had caught it that night as the car went over the bridge and into town. The streets had been bright as day and choked with cars and bikes and motorcycles, with people pushing toward the boardwalk. For a while they had sat there, trapped in traffic, as her father drummed his fingers on the steering wheel and talked about pleasure palaces and pavilions of sin.

Finally he managed to work his way over to the curb, stopping the car and leaning across to open the door. "You big girls get on up there to the boardwalk now, while Liddy, Warren, and I head for the north end of town, where the hotels and condominiums are. And we'll meet you back on this corner at ten o'clock sharp." He reached down to the floor and pulled up a cardboard box, thrusting it at Lucy as she got out of the car. "Take these here flyers and hand them out in the sweet name of Jesus," he said. "Stand up there proud on the boardwalk and speak out against Satan and tell him he's trespassing on God's property. Praise the Lord."

"Praise the Lord," whispered Lucy and Doris as they stood on the corner, holding the cardboard box between them and watching their father drive away.

"I can't go up there," said Doris. "I just can't, is all."

"Me neither," said Lucy. But even as she said it she looked toward the boardwalk at the top of the street and moved her feet in time to the music that poured down around her. Just then a group of people came by, hurrying and jostling each other, calling back and forth, and all of a sudden Lucy wanted to run along with them. She shoved the box at Doris and said, "Come on, let's go." And when her sister stood there, frozen on the corner, she went back and took her by the sleeve and pulled her forward.

They stood at the top of the ramp, caught in the wind and the swirl of people and the rumble of the boardwalk train. From somewhere out in front came the pounding of the surf, and overhead, kites swooped and danced against the darkened sky. Lights from the shops and rides and shooting galleries blazed out over the boardwalk and the air smelled of the sea and of cotton candy.

"It's beautiful," said Lucy. And she pinched her arms hard to make sure she was awake. After a while she steered Doris through the crowd to the other side of the boardwalk. "We'll set up here on this bench and do like Pa said, stand up proud for the Lord and hand out these flyers, and then after that we'll have till ten o'clock just for us. Just for looking around."

Lucy held out a flyer to a man in a yellow sweatshirt, but he pushed on past her. She tried to give one to a woman pushing a stroller, to a girl eating an Italian ice, to a boy with a Boogie board, but they all looked the other way and kept on walking. She watched a group of boys wrestling on the beach just below the boardwalk and thought how it would be time to meet her father before they even managed to give away any of the flyers. Then she reached into the box for a whole handful, fanning them out and waving them overhead. Just then, the wind caught them and carried them up and made them flap and flutter like giant seabirds before it dropped them down on the boys rolling in the sand.

"Hey, what's this?" cried one of the boys, taller than the rest and with spiky yellow hair. "What're you doing up there?"

"It's not us. It was the wind that did it," said Lucy.

"Yeah, sure. Tell me about it. You want to make our acquaintance, just say so, right, guys?" said the boy. "I'm Phil and that's Joe and this here's Matt." He held a flyer up to the light and read, in a singsong voice, "Church of the Saving Grace—Signs, Wonders, Miracles . . .' Hey, I could use me some of them wonders. Some of them miracles. How about you guys?"

"Yeah," said the other two as they leaned to read over his shoulder before all three of them jumped up onto the boardwalk, pressing close to the girls.

"How come you're dressed like that? You nuns or something?" said Phil.

"No," said Lucy, looking down and pulling her coat tight around her shiny blue dress.

"What are you, then?"

"We're—I don't know. I'm Lucy and this is Doris and she's my sister."

"What's the matter—she can't talk? You can't talk, sister Doris?"

"Yes, sure, I'm Doris."

"Doris and Lucy," said Matt.

"Lucy and Doris from the Church of the Saving Grace," said Joe.

"Loosey Lucy," said Phil. "You loose, Lucy?"

"No. I don't think—I mean, no."

"Awwww, Lucy's not loosey anymore," he said. "You from around here, then?"

"Out the road," said Lucy.

"Out the road? You guys know where that is?"

"Out the road," said Matt as he punched Joe in the stomach and doubled over with laughter.

"S'at Out the Road, Maryland, or Out the Road, Delaware?" said Phil.

"Maryland," said Lucy, looking down suddenly at the boardwalk, sure, somehow, that it was a question that wasn't meant to be answered. "Just over the bridge and down the first road on the left. It's where Pa has his church and he brought us into town to hand out these flyers, only nobody wants any."

"D'you hear that?" said Phil, grabbing a handful of flyers

21

and holding the box out to Matt and Joe. "Loosey Lucy says they got flyers that ain't gonna fly. That nobody wants. You want to see how bad they want them? You want to see?" He nodded to Matt and Joe and the three of them stepped out into the stream of people moving down the boardwalk. "Yo, citizens," he yelled as they pushed flyers at people's faces and down into beach bags and tote bags and shopping bags; as they made them into airplanes and sailed them up and into the wind.

"You see that?" said Phil, putting the empty box on Matt's head and slapping it with the flat of his hand. "That's how bad they want them. Now you gonna show us about those signs and wonders and miracles?"

"We can't," said Lucy, "on account of that's what Pa does at the tent service."

"On account of that's what Pa does," mimicked Phil. "You hear that, guys? The nun-girls can't show us nothing, but that's no never mind. We'll show them. We'll show 'em all there is to see." And he put one arm around Lucy and one arm around Doris and pushed them out into the crowd and down the boardwalk, calling over his shoulder for Matt and Joe to hurry up. They stopped in front of the Purple Cow and waited until Joe came out carrying beers in plastic cups. They went to stand under the Ferris wheel, watching as it swung round and round. "I can't believe I'm really here," said Lucy. "And not on the other side of the bay, just thinking about it."

"You're here, all right, nun-girl. Now drink up," said Phil, shoving one of the cups at her. "Before the po-lice nail us for drinking on the boardwalk."

"No," said Lucy. "It smells awful—like baby throw-up." She pushed his hand away and moved over to the Tilt-A-Whirl, closing her eyes and trying to imagine what it would feel like to be locked in a cage and tossed wildly from side to side. She opened her eyes to see Phil leaning toward her, holding his cup over her head. "This here's Milwaukee's finest and you're saying it smells like baby barf. You just got to get used to it, that's all." Lucy dodged and the beer splashed on the ground.

"Cripes, you spilled it," said Phil, chasing her around the back of the merry-go-round and down to where Doris and Matt and Joe were still standing by the Ferris wheel. He caught her by the waist and spun her around. "You spilled it and you got to pay the consequences. What'll we do with her, guys?"

"Nothing," said Lucy. "On account of it's almost ten o'clock and Pa'll be waiting for us down on the corner."

"Awwww, Pa's gonna be waiting for them. We might maybe have to let 'em go if Pa's gonna be waiting to take 'em back out the road," said Phil.

Doris and Lucy started down the boardwalk with the boys walking behind them, stepping close to their heels and catching the hems of their coats as they billowed in the wind. When they got to the ramp leading down to the street, the boys stopped and pulled them back. "You coming again?" said Phil. " 'Cause we're gonna be here all weekend."

"We might," said Lucy. She yanked her coattail free and started down the ramp.

"Maybe tomorrow," said Doris. "On account of Pa said we'd be coming into town Friday and Saturday both, to stand up for the Lord and speak out against Satan."

"We'll be waiting for you, then," called Phil. "And for some of them signs and wonders and miracles, too."

When their father dropped them off the next night, Lucy and Doris went back to the same spot on the boardwalk, sitting on the same bench, with the box of flyers between them, waiting and looking out into the crowd.

"Yo, nun-girls," they heard after a while and turned to see Phil and Matt and Joe racing across the beach. The boys jumped up onto the boardwalk and slid to a stop in front of the bench.

"So, didn't you learn nothing last night?" said Phil as he brought his hand down hard on the box of flyers. "Go on, Matt. Show 'em how it's done."

Lucy watched as Matt reached for the box and held it high before sinking it with two hands into the litter basket.

"What'll Pa say?" gasped Doris.

"What'll Pa say?" repeated Phil.

Just as Lucy was about to reach for the box, someone threw a milk shake in on top of it and she saw the chocolate liquid oozing down inside and spreading over the flyers.

"Pa'll never know, that's what," said Phil. "Now come on while we got us some time." And he caught Lucy's hand and pulled her along the boardwalk.

They waited in line for French fries and rode the Ferris wheel and the Wild Mouse. They staggered away from the Tilt-A-Whirl and ate cotton candy, peeling pink strands of sugar off each other's faces. They posed in front of mirrors, watching themselves grow tall and skinny, then short and fat, and for a minute it seemed to Lucy that she was the kind of girl she used to see in school—the kind of girl who was always laughing and having fun and who didn't have to hurry home as soon as classes were over. Because Pa said so. The kind of girl she sometimes, secretly, wanted to be.

Lucy leaned on a counter and watched as Phil threw plastic balls at garbage cans with popping-up lids.

"Oh, look at the dogs," she said, pointing to a row of dogs with long floppy ears and *Ocean City, Maryland* in red letters on their sides. "They're so cute."

"I'll win you one," said Phil. "Stick around and I'll win you one."

"We can't," said Lucy. She pointed to the clock on the boardwalk. "It's almost ten and Pa'll be waiting for us. We've got to go."

"What're you, some kind of freakin' Cinderella?" said Phil, his voice suddenly dark and angry. "After all this and you're gonna run out on us. There's a name for girls like you."

"I can't help it," said Lucy, looking up at the row of dogs, who seemed to beckon to her from the top shelf. "We have to, is all."

"Lucy's right," whispered Doris.

"Lucy's right," taunted Phil. "So go on and go, then." He picked up a ball and spit on it and made as if to throw before catching himself. "I'm gonna win one of them dogs, though, so you could just think about coming back." He threw the ball so hard that it ricocheted against the wall and dropped down into a trough.

"We can't," said Lucy. "We never could. And, besides, Pa'd skin us alive."

Phil picked up another ball and stood tossing it from one hand to the next. He looked at Lucy, at Doris, then turned away. "Nun-girls ain't worth it," he said, "except I'm going to win me this dog and I been thinking we should maybe get us a little religion. How we should maybe pay us an after-hours visit to the Church of the Saving Grace. You gonna be there?"

"We live there," said Lucy.

"Cripes—I *know* you live there, but are you gonna *be* there? For us, I mean."

"We'll be there," said Lucy, wishing her voice didn't sound so small and thready.

"Let me get this straight, then," said Phil. "Out the highway to the first road on the left."

"Just follow the signs," said Lucy as she grabbed hold of Doris and started down the boardwalk.

Lucy slid off the pickup truck and worked her way through the cars and up the road toward the tent, hearing her father's voice as it reached out into the night.

"I'm set to tell you about a God that loves the harlot," cried Preacher Peale. "About a God who loves the Jezebel. About a God who'll take that Jezebel and turn her life around. And later tonight we're going to see someone come forward and hold her sin up high and—"

"No," said Lucy. She pushed off from the side of the tent, tripped over a guy line, and sprawled on the ground, feeling the grit and stones beneath her hands. "I can't," she said as she picked herself up and raced toward the house. "I don't *care* what Pa says. I just can't."

Three

"Glory be. Praise the Lord. Hallelujah." The stupid parrot started soon's I pushed the door open and went inside.

"Shut up," I hollered as I raced up the steps and into my room. I pulled the shades down and turned on the light and took a laundry bag from the back of the door, dumping the dirty clothes in a heap on the floor and shoving clean ones in their place. I rooted in the closet for my white plastic purse—the one I got at a sidewalk sale in Virginia year before last—and opened it to make sure my seven dollars were still inside. I grabbed a jacket and went to stand by the door, looking back at the room and thinking how there ought to be something else I should take: something I should *want* to take. But there wasn't and all of a sudden there not being anything made me feel sad and sort of empty and I tiptoed into Ma and Pa's room and found a curled-up picture of me and Doris tacked up on the wall and put it in my pocket as I went down the stairs.

"Praise the Lord," squawked the parrot.

"Praise the Lord," I answered him back, mostly, I think, 'cause I couldn't leave without saying something to somebody. Even if it was a beady-eyed bird all worn and shiny like an old chair cushion. I turned away, then back again, going across the room and opening the door to the cage. "Come on," I said. "We'll go together, but once we're out of here, you're on your own. I'm warning you." I could've saved my breath, though, 'cause the stupid bird moved to the far side of the cage, and when I reached in for him he pecked me on the finger.

"Stay there, then, and see if I care," I said, pulling back and closing the door, sucking on my hand. "Except maybe you could've been halfway to Ocean City by now. If you even remember how to fly."

"Praise the Lord," said the bird.

Out on the road, I ran until my side hurt and my breath came in ragged spurts and the strings of the laundry bag dug deep into my hands. I stopped next to a field and looked over my shoulder, peering into the dark and listening hard to the sounds around me. Branches stirred overhead and from somewhere in the distance a dog barked. I thought about what was happening back at the tent and for a minute it was as if I could see Pa standing up in front of the congregation and calling out in a voice that was shouting-loud, "Now's what we've been waiting for. Now's the time for the Jezebel to come forth and speak out and shame the

Devil." I knew they'd all be waiting there—Ma, Doris, Liddy, and Warren; the men and women leaning forward in their chairs, fanning themselves with cardboard fans that said *Church of the Saving Grace* across the front.

"And mostly Pa," I said out loud. "Mostly Pa waiting there for me on account of he promised me to them like a double coupon at the Dollar General. Only when I'm not there to do all that coming forth and speaking out and shaming—then what'll he do?" Suddenly I had a picture in my head of Pa stopping the service flat out and setting off down the road after me and I threw the laundry bag over my shoulder and started to run, not daring to look back till I reached the highway.

When I got to the bridge I stopped and leaned against the rail to catch my breath. Cars rumbled past behind me and I felt a whoosh of air on the backs of my legs. "Draw's set to go up any minute now," said a fisherman beside me. "So if you're fixing to head on into town you'd better go, else you'll wait a spell." And I took up my belongings again and hightailed it across the bridge, getting to the other side just as the bell rang and the draw rose slowly toward the sky.

I went through the town and up onto the boardwalk on account of that's the only place I knew *to* go. But instead of heading for the rides and all I turned the other way and found an empty bench and sort of collapsed down on it and listened to the ocean and the *shlush shlush shlush* of people going past in back of me. After a while I dropped down onto the beach and crawled under the boardwalk, punching my laundry bag into a pillow and wrapping my jacket tight around me. The last thing I remember was digging my fingers into the sand before I slept.

I woke the next morning with sand in my hair and a crick in my neck. Besides that, I had to go to the bathroom. For a few minutes I just lay there listening to the bikes going by overhead and watching the light through the boardwalk. Then I came out on the beach, pushing and pulling at my clothes and trying to look like I'd slept some place *real*. The sun was already high in the sky and I headed down toward the concessions, checking to make sure my money was still there and thinking how a cup of tea might stop the squishy feeling in my stomach. It wasn't long before the sweet greasy smell of waffles and sausage and saltwater taffy closed over me like some giant fishing net and I turned and fought my way out from under and down a side street, where I sat on the curb and told myself I would *not* throw up.

Farther along the avenue, I found the bus depot and went in to use the bathroom. Afterwards I scrubbed my hands and face and armpits with a paper towel, trying not to see the slime and gunk that looked like it'd been floating in the sink forever. When I was done, I stood for a minute leaning on the windowsill. Just then a car pulled onto the parking lot. It was old and dented and a funny metallic blue. Like Pa's car. I jumped back away from the window and stood for a minute, holding my breath. When I looked again a teenage boy was just getting out of the car and I watched as he waved to a girl and, after a minute, the two of them got in and drove away.

It was right strange but when I went outside and stood on the parking lot and looked at where the car had been I knew, sure as anything, that Pa wasn't coming after me: that he'd meant it when he said unless I came forward at the service I was no kin of his ever again. And I didn't care. Except that I did. And I felt suddenly alone.

I got myself a Coke out of a machine and went to sit on a little pier behind a row of weathered gray houses back on the bayside of Ocean City, holding the can up to my face, feeling the cold burn against my skin. I took a mouthful, tasting the prickles, and swallowed carefully to keep from throwing up. I thought about the baby that might maybe be growing inside of me. I thought about how I couldn't be pregnant—not just from doing it the once, and about how babies were supposed to happen with somebody you loved—with somebody who loved you back. And not with a he-turkey like Phil.

And all of a sudden I couldn't keep from thinking about that night and it was like I was in the Tilt-A-Whirl up on the boardwalk with the sky and the water and the pier going every which way around me. I held tight to a piling and leaned my head against it.

Doris and I had waited till the house was quiet, till Liddy clean talked herself out and Pa was snoring like a buzz saw. Then we'd got up, dressed, and climbed through the bathroom window onto the shed roof and down to the ground. We stood in the shadow of the tent, half scared that Phil and Matt and Joe would actually show up; half scared they wouldn't. Just when we were fixing to go back inside, a car turned in off the road, blinking its lights before going dark.

"It's them. They're here—do you think?" said Doris, catching hold of me. And together we stood there, hanging on to each other, listening to the slam of the car door, the sound of glass against glass, a rustling, a scuffling.

"Yo, nun-girls, 's'at you?" called Phil as the boys came up the road, Matt and Joe carrying a cooler between them.

"Shhhh," said Doris.

"Shhhh yourself," said Phil.

"Pa'll *hear* you," I said.

"Pa'll *hear* you," said Phil. He dug in the cooler and pulled out a couple of bottles, flipping the caps before he held them out to Doris and me. I took a taste and the drink was thick and sweet and burned my throat. "What is it?" I said when I was sure I could speak again.

"Pepsi," said Phil.

"Not like any Pepsi I've ever had before," I said, taking another swallow, and then another.

"Holy water, then." He reached in the cooler for a beer and stood back, looking up at the tent in the moonlight. "So this' where all them signs and wonders and miracles take place," he said. "Let's go inside."

"No, stop. You can't." I pulled at his arm, feeling it all hard and ropy under my fingers. "That's Pa's. Besides, it's a church."

"With angel statues? And an altar at the front?"

"Not like that, but it's a church just the same. Mostly with folding chairs and a platform where Pa stands to preach and to call for the sinners to come forward."

"He's not in there, is he? Pa, I mean?"

"No," I said. "But still—"

"Leave it, Phil," said Matt.

We all stood there, sort of in a circle, not moving and watching Phil, wondering what he would do next. After a minute he shrugged and spit on the ground. "So who cares about Pa anyways," he said. "We've come to get some of what *you* got to offer."

"What's that?" I said, then wished I could swallow back the words.

"What's that?" yelled Phil. "What's *that*? Loosey Lucy wants to know what's that." He came close to me and put his arm around my shoulder, turning me away from the tent. "Come on down to the car so maybe I can think of something. Besides that, I got a present for you."

"No, I can't," I said, and I started in to think about all the things I'd heard in the girls' bathroom at school—about what some boys are like—the stuff they do.

"A present, Lucy," Phil said. "You want a present, you know you do." He pulled at me and I pulled back. But then I didn't anymore, on account of my head feeling all warm and dreamy. And we went on down the road, me picking each foot up high to keep from tripping.

"Where's the present?" I said when we got to the car.

"Not so fast, nun-girl. Gotta have a little something more to drink." And he reached in his back pocket and took out a bottle, pouring some of what was in it into my Pepsi. "Gotta get in the car first," said Phil, opening the door and pushing me from behind until I climbed into the back seat. The car was hot and dark and it took a while before I could make out the shape of Phil sitting next to me. I drank some of my Pepsi but it didn't taste as good as it had before, so I swallowed it down quick and felt it burn clear to the bottoms of my feet.

"Okay, you ready for what I got for you?" said Phil. "You ready for the present?"

And all of a sudden I felt scared and excited both at the same time. "Yes," I said. "Oh, yes."

"Yes, oh, yes," said Phil, sounding more like me than I'd sounded myself. Then he leaned over the front seat, grabbing for something, turning on the light, and holding up a white fuzzy dog with *Ocean City, Maryland* in red letters along the side.

"See—I said I'd win you one and I did. Now what do you say to that?"

"Thank you," I said, reaching for the dog.

"You gotta do better than that."

"Thank you, Phil."

"Better'n 'Thank you, Phil.' "

"Thank you, Phil, a whole heap." I held the toy dog up against my face, liking the way it felt cool and soft.

"Hey, can I have me some of that?" he said and I moved the dog over his face and neck.

"Not with the toy, dammit, the real thing," and he took the dog and hurled it up into the front seat, so that it bounced off the dashboard and landed on the steering wheel. He leaned close and rubbed against me, the hair on his cheek making my cheek feel raw and itchy. He dropped his beer can out the window and threw my Pepsi after it. "We don't need that anymore," he said as he pushed his mouth against my mouth, his tongue against my tongue, all the while pulling at my dress, my slip, my underpants.

"No," I cried. "No, you shouldn't ought to do this." But he was on me then, pressing against me, catching at my hands. And he was heavy.

Afterwards I just lay there with the seat belt digging into my back and the smell of Phil all around me. Then I was out of the car, shaking but sort of numb, too. What I knew more'n anything was that I wanted to get away from there, from Phil, and up to where Doris was waiting for me. I fixed my clothes as best I could and I started up the road, stumbling and even falling the once, running.

"Yo, nun-girl," I heard from somewhere in back of me and I turned just as Phil sent the toy dog sailing through the air. "There—don't say I never gave you anything."

Without even thinking, I reached out, caught the dog, and kept on going to where Doris and Matt and Joe were sitting around the cooler chest.

After a spell Matt and Joe picked up their cooler and went down to where Phil waited by the car, saying they wanted to get into town, it being their last night and all. Then Doris and I went back across the shed roof and in the bathroom window and through the night-still house. I fell in bed, feeling hot and shamed and cold and dirty all at the same time, staring at the outline of the window, trying not to think. But still I kept wondering about things, about what happened—did I let it happen? Or was it all to do with Phil? *Phil*, a voice screamed out inside of me. *Phil Phil Phil.* And more than anything I wanted to talk to Doris. But I couldn't. I couldn't. Then, tired as I was, I got up and took that dog and stuffed him under the rafters in the back of my closet, saying to myself how I never wanted to see it ever again. Or Phil neither.

I looked up to see a woman standing at the end of the pier and I sort of somehow had the feeling she'd been standing there awhile.

"Are you all right?" she said. And it wasn't till she asked that I realized I was crying.

"Yes, ma'am," I said. "I'm fine. It's just that—you know—" I blinked to show her how it was the sun that was making my eyes water.

"You're sure?" she went on. "Because you look as if you could use someone to talk to." I nodded and shook my head both at the same time, wishing all the while that I could tell her I wasn't sure at all: that I rightly *could* use someone to talk to. But I didn't, though, and instead I picked up my bag and mumbled something about looking for the laundromat.

When I stood there like I didn't know which way to go she said, "The laundromat's on the next street over and to the north. Just past the library."

And I felt her watching after me all the way up the street and till I turned the corner.

Four

Lucy sat at the table in the library, looking out into the room without seeing it, and trying to think of what to do next. "A job," she told herself. "I've got to get me a job. And a place to stay. Or a place to stay and *then* a job." But the more she tried to concentrate, the more her thoughts seemed to break away and disappear, like fiddler crabs burrowing back into the sand.

She got up and started around the library, running her fingers along the shelves, spinning the racks of paperbacks, opening the drawers of the card catalogue. She stood at the window for a minute, watching the stream of people outside heading for the beach, then moved on past the newspapers and magazines to the reference section. "A B C D, E F G," she sang the alphabet song inside her head, tapping the spine of each volume of the encyclopedia as she went along, speeding up on "L M N O P" and slowing to a drag on "W X and Y and Z." All of a sudden she grabbed "B" and "P" off the shelf and held them tight against her chest as she hurried back to her place.

Lucy opened the "B" book flat on the table, leafing through the pages until she found what she was looking for. There was a whole section on "Baby." There were pictures of a baby crawling and playing with her toes—in a bathtub, a high chair, a car seat. There was a baby with a mother and father, leaning close and looking at her as if there were nothing else to look at in the whole entire world. Lucy blinked and tried to imagine her own face where the book mother's was. She closed her eyes and tried to put Phil in the place of the book father—but nothing happened. She opened her eyes and closed them again, washed over with a sudden cold because she knew, sure as she knew anything, that she couldn't remember what Phil looked like. She slammed the book hard, pinching her finger and glad for the pain.

After a while she opened the book again and started to read, whispering the words just under her breath. She read about bathing, fresh air, and sleeping conditions; about feeding, clothing, and handling the baby. But there's nothing here to tell me if I've got me one, she thought. Nothing that tells about the throwing-up feeling in my stomach and how I'm sore up top and not as flat as I used to be. Lucy put the book aside and took up volume "P," glancing over her shoulder to see if anyone was watching her. She looked for "Pregnant" and found "Pregnancy" but there was only a notation to "*See* Gestation, Embryo." She put her head down on the book, watching the print blur before her eyes, and thought that there had to be something, somewhere, that would tell her what she needed to know.

"Except maybe I don't," she said, catching her breath and biting down hard on her lower lip when she realized she had spoken out loud. "Except maybe I don't need to know," she went on to herself. "On account of it could all be a mistake and tomorrow or next week I'll get my period again and everything'll be the way it was meant to be." But suddenly she felt trapped, as if the stacks, the shelves, the paperback racks were inching closer, crowding around her. She took the books and jumped up, going over to the shelf and pushing the "B" and the "P" in so hard that they hit the wall in back. Then she grabbed a *Seventeen* off the magazine rack and sat down in a chair by the window.

For a minute Lucy watched a group of girls outside, waiting for the light to change so they could cross the street. They were sleek and tan, all with long blond hair, and Lucy was sure their voices, if she could hear them, would sound like wind through the trees. She tugged at a strand of her own dark hair, winding it around her finger, then letting it fall lank and straight. She stuck her legs out in front of her, staring down at her skin, flat and white and massed with freckles. She rubbed her hand in a circular motion over her stomach. Then she opened the magazine and suddenly it was as though the girls who had been outside were inside now, caught there in the pages of *Seventeen* like flies on sticky paper.

Lucy put her head back and listened to the rhythm of the copying machine. There was a hush of voices and, from outside, the sound of church bells playing "Amazing Grace." For the first time since she left home, she felt safe. She could almost imagine herself living in the library forever, spending the days looking at pictures in the books that lined the walls, hiding in the bathroom at closing time, coming out at night to curl up in a corner or on one of the beanbag chairs over in the children's section. She turned and watched as a girl went by, pushing a cart of books. I could do that, she thought to herself. And for a minute she saw herself going along, replacing books on shelves, straightening magazines, pushing chairs back into the tables.

"I could do that," Lucy heard herself say as she stood facing the librarian across the desk. "What that girl's doing, with the books on the cart. I could do that."

"I'm sure you could," said the librarian. "The only trouble is that we already have Liz, and a young man named Dave, who do it for us. They're local and work part time year round and then we take them on full time in the summer. Are you looking for a job?"

"Yes, ma'am," said Lucy. "I guess."

"Oh, dear," said the librarian, spreading a stack of cards out on the desk in front of her. "Have you been looking long? There's generally a turnover. Someone quits, there's a vacancy. There'll be a 'Help Wanted' sign in a window or posted on a door. In fact, I saw one this morning in the pizza place next to the laundromat. Or try the employment office in town—five blocks down and on the left."

"Thank you," said Lucy, stepping back and bumping into the card catalogue. She turned and hunched her shoulders, willing the librarian not to ask her any questions. But she knows anyway, thought Lucy as she hurried across the room, reaching for her bag and heading for the door. I reckon she knows about the encyclopedia, about "Baby" and "Pregnant" and what I was looking to find out and how I'm not meant to be here and slept under the boardwalk and everything else besides. On account of this's a library and she's a librarian and maybe librarians *know* these things.

Lucy stood looking at the sign in the window of the pizza place, running her finger over the glass and tracing the orange fluorescent letters. HELP WANTED. "Help wanted," she whispered under her breath. "Help wanted, help wanted. Help." She opened the door and breathed in the thick warmth of cheese, tomatoes, and peppers. A radio was playing and the music pulsed against the walls, bouncing off the plate-glass window in front. Two girls leaned against the counter, talking to the boy who worked there.

"Help you?" he called, speaking into the sudden lull between the music and the commercial. "Help you?"

Help wanted, thought Lucy. Help wanted. The words throbbed inside of her but she shook her head and backed slowly out of the store.

The employment office was small and cramped and smelled of ashtrays. There was a man sitting at a desk, leaning forward and playing both sides of a chess game. "In a minute," he mumbled, without looking up, as he continued to stare down at the board. Lucy shifted from one foot to the next. She cleared her throat and wound the strings of the laundry bag around her fingers. She watched the fan on the file cabinet as it swung slowly away, then back again, ruffling the calendar on the wall with every return trip. Suddenly the man seemed to pounce, leaning across the board and snatching up one of the pieces from the other side. Then he got up and moved deliberately around the desk to look at what he had done.

Slouching back in his chair, he turned to Lucy and said, "Are you looking for work?"

"Yes," said Lucy. She dropped her bag and kicked it aside, wishing suddenly that she was sleek and tan, with long blond hair—the way all the other girls in Ocean City seemed to be. "Something. Anything."

"Anything?" The man studied her for a minute before turning back to the chessboard. "There's some construction work out there. Dry walls and stuff. But I guess that's not your bag."

"No," said Lucy, "maybe something less—something more—"

"Don't worry," he said, opening the desk drawer and taking out a piece of paper. "Stuff'll be coming in. It's near the end of summer and some of these kids'll be getting tired, thinking about heading home. Just last week we had a call for a spook up at the spook house on the boardwalk. Morbid Mansion, it's called. You should've been here for that one."

"I guess," said Lucy, tugging at her dress and smoothing her hair and wondering why he thought she would have fit in at something called Morbid Mansion.

"Well, anyway, fill this out and we'll keep it on file for when something does come in. Name, address, and telephone number. Social Security number, too."

Lucy looked down at the application he held out to her. She started to reach for it, but the words swam in front of her, dipping and wavering there on the page. She felt light-headed and suddenly hungry and caught herself on the edge of the desk.

"Hey—you okay?" the man asked.

Lucy stepped hard on the instep of one foot with the heel of the other and concentrated on the form he still held in front of her. The word "Address" seemed to grow and grow until she thought it would burst. "Later. I'll come back later," she said as she pushed her way out the door into the heat and sunshine.

The rest of the afternoon went by in a jumble. Lucy sat for a while on the edge of the boardwalk, watching the kites. She took off her shoes and walked along the beach, dragging her laundry bag behind her and looking over her shoulder at the smooth swath it cut in the sand. She stood on the jetty, facing out to sea, but the pounding of the waves made her feel suddenly small and she turned and hurried back over rocks that were cool and gritty to her feet. She watched a child building a castle and wrote the word "job" in the sand with her big toe, then stood back as the water washed over it and swallowed it away.

She headed across the beach and crawled under the boardwalk to hide her things behind a clump of driftwood; coming out into the sunlight, she sat down on the sand, her back against a piling. I have to get a job, but I can't get a job until I have a room and I'll never have a room until I get a job, on account of maybe they'll ask me to pay in advance. Lucy shook her head, trying to clear her mind, but the thoughts stuck to it like burrs to a dog's ear.

A man came by, selling ice cream, and she jumped up and went after him. She dug money out of her purse for a

Chipwich and stood there peeling the paper away and nibbling the edge of one of the cookies. For a minute she held the taste of chocolate in her mouth, then she bit into the middle part. Again, and again, gobbling it down and ignoring the pain in the roof of her mouth from the cold. She licked her lips, her fingers, and the inside of the paper wrapper. And when there was nothing left to eat, Lucy was hungrier than she had ever been before. Her mouth watered and her insides twisted. Her stomach growled and rumbled and roared.

Lucy ran up onto the boardwalk, reaching into her wallet and counting the money that was left. For a minute she saw herself spreading the dollars out on the nearest counter, asking for fries and pizza, maybe a shake. She caught herself, stopping just as she got to the Alaska stand. "No," she said, biting down hard on the word. "That's for tomorrow, and the day after, and maybe the day after that."

She stood for a minute with the people swirling around her and all of a sudden it seemed to Lucy that everyone was eating something: burgers and Belgian waffles and chocolate-covered bananas; cookies and caramel corn. Mouths opened and closed: biting, chewing, licking. She turned and dropped down onto a bench next to a woman with a tub of French fries. "I shouldn't do this," the woman said, looking at Lucy. "These're definitely *not* on my diet, but sometimes, you know, at the beach . . . Oh, it's worth it." She dangled a long, thin strip of potato from her fingers, then reached out and caught it with her tongue, moaning softly. Lucy's mouth watered and she swallowed hard. "No," said the woman, snapping her mouth shut and waiting awhile before going on. "I won't. That's enough.

You know what they say—a minute on the lips, forever on the hips." And she jumped up and moved off, setting the tub carefully on the top of the heaped-up trash in the overflowing litter basket. Lucy followed right along behind her, scooping up the box, turning quickly, and heading in the other direction, not stopping until she was sure the woman hadn't seen, wasn't coming after her. Then she stood in front of the mirror outside the fun house, watching herself grow short and round as she ate the fries, savoring the salty, vinegary taste and hoping they would never end.

Lucy was surprised to see that it was night, that the lights were on, the sky dark overhead. She leaned on a rail at the end of the boardwalk, looking out at the inlet and feeling heavy and tired. After a while she turned back into the crowd and allowed herself to be carried along, attaching herself first to one group and then to another, pretending that she belonged: that she was somebody's sister or cousin or aunt.

Farther on, under a sign that read *Tin Can Alley*, a crowd spilled out onto the boardwalk and Lucy stopped, pressing forward, standing on tiptoe. The lights, the music, the cartoon cats popping up out of garbage cans, the clanking of the lids, were all suddenly familiar. She wanted to turn and run, but she felt her feet inching forward, her body twisting through the wall of people until she was close to the front. A boy stood by the counter. He was thin and not too tall, with bristly eyebrows and a Baltimore Orioles cap backward on his head. As she watched, he picked up a ball and threw it, landing it safely inside the purple can just as the lid fell shut.

The numbers clicked and changed on the tote board overhead. A cheer went up from the crowd.

"You're almost there, Jake."

"Go for it, man."

The boy turned slowly, bowing and wiping his hands down the sides of his jeans. "Ocean City today—tomorrow the world," he said as he swung back, reaching for another ball and hurtling it through the air in a flash.

Lights blazed. The man working the stand pushed a button and the cats in the cans popped up, bobbling there, nodding and shaking their heads before they disappeared again and the lids clanged down.

"That's it. You did it," the man said. "In Vegas they'd say you done broke the bank." He plucked a white stuffed dog with floppy ears and the words *Ocean City, Maryland* along the side off the top shelf and handed it to the boy.

Lucy let out a cry.

The boy turned. And for a moment they stood looking at each other.

"Here," he said, holding out the dog. "You want it? I mean—I—it's, you know, the winning that counts."

But Lucy was already fighting against the crowd, pushing her way out. "No," she yelled. "No. No. No."

As she ran across the boardwalk she heard the sound of laughter pouring up out of the crowd.

"Way to go, Jake."

"You sure have a way with women."

"Tell us your secret—or maybe don't tell us."

Lucy jumped down onto the beach and kept on going until she was almost to the water's edge. She stood on the hard wet sand and fought to get her breath. She stared out at the dark ocean in front of her and tried not to think.

"Hey, are you all right?" She heard the voice from somewhere in back of her and without thinking stepped forward into a wave and felt the water splatter the hem of her dress and wash down into her shoes.

"What is it with you?" The boy named Jake caught her by the elbow and pulled her back. "I mean, I may not be Mel Gibson, but I don't usually send people running, not into the drink, anyway."

Lucy broke away and went up the beach, sitting on the edge of an overturned lifeguard stand and pulling off her shoes, shoving her feet down into the sand. "Who's Mel Gibson?" she said after a while.

"Who's *Mel Gibson?*" said Jake. "Mel Gibson is—you know, in the movies and all. Mel Gibson is who'd never send girls running. Not *away* from him, anyway."

"He would if they thought he was somebody else," said Lucy.

"Is that what you thought? That I was somebody else?"

"I maybe did."

"Must've been King Kong you were expecting, then," said Jake. He moved to sit on the other end of the lifeguard stand, but when he saw Lucy tense and draw herself up as if to run again, he dropped down, cross-legged, where he was and shaped the sand in front of him into a kind of barricade. "There," he said. "Safe as pockets, as my mother always says."

"Safe as pockets." Lucy whispered the words. Then suddenly she was crying. Great tearing sobs that seemed to come from her feet, that caught in her throat and shook her body. She doubled over and put her head on her knees, rocking back and forth. After a while she looked up and blinked in the light from the boardwalk. She peered at Jake where he still sat in his circle of sand, wiped her nose on the hem of her dress, and didn't say anything.

"You could give a guy a complex," he said. "With the running and the crying and . . ."

"It's not to do with you," said Lucy. "The crying, anyways. It's just that when you said that, about being safe as pockets—only I'm not—it made me feel sad. And sort of—"

"Lonely?"

"Yeah, lonely."

Jake took off his cap and shoved it down in his belt. He ran his fingers through his dark blond hair and said, "Okay, so now let's begin again. I'm Jake. Jake Jarrett." He waited a minute and when Lucy didn't say anything he went on. "Now's when you're supposed to say, 'I'm Jane, or Sue, or Anastasia.' "

"Lucy," said Lucy.

"Lucy. Lucia. I had a cat named Lucia once. A tabby. She was my sister's really, only she took me over. I broke my leg at the end of seventh grade and was laid up for the summer and we hung out together. Well, we didn't exactly hang out. I was stuck there on the couch reading Sherlock Holmes and she sat on my cast and slept. But I guess for a cat that's hanging out. Do you like cats?"

"I never had one," said Lucy. "Or any other pet, except for a mean-spirited parrot that belonged to my mother, and then when I offered to let it go free the fool thing bit me."

"Recently?" said Jake.

"What recently?" said Lucy.

"Did he bite you recently? The mean-spirited parrot."

"How come you want to know?"

Jake shrugged and said, "It's just a roundabout way of asking if you're new in town."

"How come you want to know *that*?"

"Because that's what people say. 'New in town?' 'Where're you from?' 'Where do you work?' Any of the above. So—are you? New in town?"

"I reckon," said Lucy.

"How long?"

"Since yesterday."

"That's new. Where're you staying?"

"You ask a lot of questions," said Lucy, sliding off the lifeguard stand to sit in the sand, leaning back against it.

"Yep," said Jake. "It's how I find things out. Besides, I know it's hard sometimes. Coming into town late in the season when everybody's pretty much settled, unless you're with your family, or something. I just thought—I know some kids you could maybe stay with."

"I got a place," said Lucy, feeling suddenly prickly. "I got a place. Or leastways I will. Tomorrow, or maybe the day after that."

"And meanwhile?"

"Meanwhile's no concern of yours," she said.

"Meanwhile's under the boardwalk, then. Right?"

Lucy turned away from him and dug her heels into the sand.

"Yeah, well, the rent's probably okay, but it's hell in the rain," Jake went on. "Besides, it's a stupid idea. Ocean

City's not all fun and games, you know. It's got its share of weirdos like anyplace else."

"You sound like my pa," said Lucy, remembering how her father would stand up on the platform and preach about the evils of Sin City. And for a moment she almost thought she could hear his voice, rolling up out of the waves as they slammed against the shore.

"Is that so bad? Sounding like your father?"

Lucy didn't answer him. Instead, she hunched her shoulders, willing herself not to cry again.

"Okay. I get the message. Nothing more about your accommodations *or* your father. So—how about food? You eating?"

"I ate already."

"Enough?"

"Yes," whispered Lucy as all the earlier hunger and sickness washed over her. "Now leave me be. I was doing fine till you came along."

"Yeah, great. No job. Noplace to stay. And making a scene on the boardwalk."

"It wasn't any scene," said Lucy.

"A minor scene." Then Jake was up on his feet, brushing the sand off the seat of his pants and calling over his shoulder as he started up the beach, "Don't go anywhere. I'll be right back."

And before Lucy could think about what to do next he was back, standing in front of her, the smell of food drifting out around him. "Here," he said as he leaned forward and held out a paper cup, a cardboard container.

"No," said Lucy, pulling back.

"Oh, yeah. Right. I forgot. I'm no Mel Gibson." He

moved away and put the food down on the sand, then went to sit where he had been before.

I don't want it, thought Lucy. I won't eat it. But she was already scuttling across the beach, grabbing for the box and opening it, biting into the hamburger. She tore off a hunk and shoved it in her mouth, feeling the sand from her hands grit against her teeth. She swallowed hard, but it was as if there was noplace for the food to go. She started to sweat and felt hot and cold both at the same time. Her stomach lurched. And suddenly she was up, running back toward a metal trash can, grabbing hold of it, gagging, and finally vomiting into it. Afterwards she slid down the side of the can and rested her face against the metal.

"You okay?" said Jake, coming up in back of her.

"Yes."

"Maybe you ate too fast. Especially if you haven't had anything for a while. There's a shake over there. Maybe later—after a while—"

Lucy crawled around to the other side of the can. "Just leave me be."

Jake stood without saying anything.

"Go," said Lucy.

"Okay. If you're sure. If—"

"Just go." She watched as he started across the beach, saw him stop and then come partway back.

"Listen," he said, calling over the noise of the ocean. "I'll go, if that's what you want. But I've got this place right down on Fourth Street. Two blocks back and on the left. It's called 'Summer Wind' and I'm on the second floor. If you need anything. Okay?"

Five

"Okay," said Lucy when Jake had gone across the beach and disappeared into the crowd up on the boardwalk. "Okay. Okay. If I need anything." She started to laugh, her voice catching in the wind and whipping around her. She pushed away from the trash can and sat up straight. "I'll tell you what I need—but not from you, Jake Jarrett. Not from you or Phil or from my pa. Not from the lady librarian or the man in the employment office. I need a whole heap of things. I need a bathtub and a job and food to eat that doesn't come flying back up soon's I swallow it down. I need for the world to get smaller or me to get bigger so's I'm not all the time feeling that I'm littler than I ought to be. And I need a way to get the sand out of my hair.

"And most of all I need to know if I'm growing me a

baby and what in God's green earth I'll *do* with it." She
shook her head, feeling for a moment that she was trapped
on the boardwalk carousel, going round and round past the
same old thoughts: a place to stay, a job, a baby—or maybe
not a baby. She got to her feet and went over to pick up
the milk shake that Jake had left on the beach, carrying it
down to the shoreline and drinking it slowly until there
was nothing left, until she had licked the last trace of
chocolate off the straw. As she stared out at the ocean,
Lucy saw that the waves were larger, fiercer than they had
been before and, overhead, the sky was layered with
clouds. The wind pushed and pulled at her as she turned
and fought her way back to the boardwalk, feeling the sting
of sand on her legs, her arms, her face.

There was a rumble of thunder and Lucy ducked under
the boardwalk, crouching low and waiting for a minute as
her eyes grew accustomed to the dark. Then, on hands and
knees, she inched her way to the pile of driftwood, reached
for her belongings, and hurried back the way she had come.
She sat, hugging her laundry bag against her chest, and
listened to the signs creaking in the wind and the sound
of people running for cover as the rain began in a torrent.
The thunder roared again, followed by a slash of lightning
across the sky. Lucy pulled back. She lowered her head
and pressed it hard against her knees. Water sluiced down
through the cracks and washed over her so that there was
no getting away from it. After a few minutes she got up
and scooped a hole out of the sand. She shoved her bag
down into it and sat on top of it. Like a chicken sitting on
an egg, she thought. But leastways maybe it'll stay dry.

There was another crack of thunder, closer this time,

and louder, and for a minute Lucy felt as if the ground shook beneath her. She put her hands up over her head, pushing her arms flat against her ears, but still the sound caromed around her, rolling up from the water and across the beach, bouncing off the boardwalk overhead.

"God's shaking his fist." She shaped the words and spoke them in a whisper, but her voice was small and lost in the noise that beat down around her. "God's shaking his fist." She heard the words again, this time in her father's voice, and suddenly she remembered a scene from her childhood. There had been a storm and she and Doris had been huddled under a bed, hanging on to each other and pressing back against the wall while her father stood in the middle of the floor and called, his voice rising above the sound of the thunder. "There's evil in the world and God's shaking his fist tonight. He's shaking it at the sinners: at the liars and the cheats and the thieves, at the harlots and the Jezebels."

"No," cried Lucy. And she jumped up, bumping her head against the post, and thought about Jake: about how he had left and come back again: about how he had told her where he lived. "For if I need anything," she said to herself. She looked at the street sign, squinting against the rain, and saw that she was only on Second Street. She turned and pushed her way into the wind as she made her way up to Fourth.

Once she was off the boardwalk, the wind was not as strong and Lucy stopped for a minute, wiping the rain out of her eyes and peeling her sodden skirt away from her legs. She hoisted her bag higher and went on, across one street and then another, wading through water over her ankles. Two blocks back and on the left is what he said, she thought. A place called "Summer Wind." She stopped again, this time to catch her breath, and looked up at the darkened cottages jumbled there one next to the other. At the end of the block she saw a light, with a sign hanging crookedly below it, and she went toward it, peering through the rain and trying to make out the words. She stood on tiptoe and reached for it as it spun crazily in the wind. She caught it and held it steady, reading the words "Summer Wind." Then, still clutching her bag, she started up the stairs to the second floor.

The windows facing onto the porch were dark. The door was closed. Rain drummed on the roof overhead and slanted in from the north, so that the chairs, the table, the pile of beer cans and the rubber fins were wet and slick. Lucy took a deep breath and tried to stop the running feeling still inside of her. She pushed a soggy beach towel out of the way and sat on the edge of a chair. She jumped up and went to the railing and stood leaning against it. She moved back to the door, but when she raised her hand to knock she found she couldn't do it and turned instead to the windows, pressing her forehead flat against the glass and trying to see inside. The dark was thick and unyielding and gave nothing back, not even her own reflection. She piled her bag on the little metal table, then watched as the whole thing collapsed in a heap on the floor. A surfboard lay propped against the wall under the windows, and almost without thinking, Lucy crawled in back of it, stretching out there and closing herself off from the world outside.

Sometime during the night the thunder and lightning receded, but the rain continued, droning against the porch roof, slapping the rail, and lashing the sides of the house. The wind, in its turn, rattled the windowpanes and caught an occasional garbage can and sent it spinning down the street. Huddled there behind the surfboard, Lucy heard all this as if from far away: part of another storm, another time. The floor was hard and scratchy with sand. Her bones ached and her arm, from resting her head on it, was numb. She stared up at the dark and willed herself to sleep, and not to sleep. She counted backward from one hundred and forward by threes. She played "I Pack My Grandmother's Trunk" and made it all the way to M for mustard before the words drifted off.

Lucy was stiff and cold when she awoke the next morning. She propped herself up on her elbow, holding tight to the surfboard with her other hand as she tilted it forward and rested her chin against it. It took a while for her eyes to adjust and at first she didn't see Jake standing at the rail, his gray sweatsuit blending with the mist, as he looked at the sky. He checked his watch and was turning to go back inside when he saw Lucy.

"It's me," she said when they had stared at each other for a minute, neither of them saying anything. "Lucy, from last night. And you said, if I needed anything—and I did." She struggled to sit up, to free herself from the surfboard.

"Here—let me." Jake jumped forward and reached for it.

"No," cried Lucy. "I can do it myself." But suddenly her arms and legs felt weak and spindly and she gave up, flopping back against the wall and watching as he lifted the board away from her and moved it to the other side of the porch.

"I'm glad to see you," he said when she had moved into a chair and sat smoothing her skirt down around her legs. "I worried about you last night." He stopped and grinned and ran his fingers through his hair. "Well, I thought about worrying about you, anyway. It was just starting to thunder when I got home and I was going back to look for you but I sat down on the bed instead—only for a minute, you understand—but I must've flaked out 'cause the next thing I knew it was morning. Except I seem to remember a lot of dreams featuring tom-toms, and big bass drums. The thunder, I guess."

"God shaking his fist," said Lucy softly.

"*What?*"

"God shaking his fist," repeated Lucy. "At the sinners."

"Who told you that?" said Jake.

"My pa."

"No way. Mine always said it was angels moving their furniture around. At least that's what he said when I was really little—then he got into wind currents and whatever thunder actually is. I always liked the furniture story better, though."

"Me, too," said Lucy. "If I knew what kind of furniture angels *have*."

"Oh, that's easy," said Jake. "Dad told me that part, too. Celestial sofas, angelic armchairs, heavenly hassocks. And don't forget the divine divan."

Lucy closed her eyes tight and for a minute she could see a whole crowd of white-robed angels pushing and shoving at chairs and tables and roly-poly footstools. "Yes," she said. "That's much better. If I'd known *that*, I might not've been afraid of the storm. Not that I was very much, mind you."

"Yeah, well, that was the point, I guess. Mom and Dad were great at teaching us how not to be afraid of things, even when there were things to be afraid *of*. And right now I have to go to work and the worst part of that is it's stopped raining just enough for the crazies to be out in force." When Lucy looked at him blankly, he explained. "The tourists. Up on the beach. I'm a lifeguard, on the Beach Patrol, and it never fails that after a storm, or during a lull, like this one, the macho types take on the ocean single-handedly and we have to pull them out." He shrugged and made a face and started for the door. "Anyway, come on inside."

"No," said Lucy, more to herself than to him, as she held tight to the arms of the chair and thought how, now that the rain had stopped, it was time for her to move on. But in a minute Jake was back, standing in front of her with a mug of coffee, offering it to her. Lucy hesitated, then reached for the mug, holding it between her hands, feeling the warmth and the steam against her face. All of a sudden, the queasy feeling in her stomach was back and she set the coffee on the railing, pushing it away as she crossed her fingers and prayed not to be sick.

Jake sat on the chair opposite her, stretching his legs out in front of him and poking at the broken table with one foot as he looked from Lucy to the mug and back to Lucy again. "Well, I got to get out of here," he said after a while. "And, unless it pours, I'll probably be gone all day, so why don't you go on inside, make yourself at home. There's stuff in the 'frigerator. At least I think there is." And when Lucy didn't say anything, he went on. "Look, it's not so bad in there. Not something the health department'd get worked up over. Not like the place where a bunch of guys and I stayed last year—a.k.a. the armpit."

"What happened to it?" said Lucy, feeling that she should say something, if only to keep the conversation going, to keep from having to think about what to do next.

"The armpit? Oh, it's still there," said Jake. "It's just that at the end of last summer when everybody else went back to college, and I decided not to, I moved into this place and then, by the time they came back *this* summer, I'd gotten sort of used to being on my own, so I just stayed put. I think, looking back, that that's what I didn't like about college. The dorm. But then my sister's always said I was old beyond my years—before my time. Well, what she really said was that I was nothing but a little old man. And she may be right." He got up, went inside, and came out a few minutes later with a towel looped around his neck and carrying a bicycle. "So, I'm off. Will you be here? When I get back?"

"I don't know," said Lucy. "But thanks."

"For what? The use of a porch? A porch, a porch, my kingdom for a porch. Or was it a horse?" he said as he bumped the bicycle down the steps, swung onto it, and started up the street. "Keep in touch, Lucia," he called back over his shoulder.

Lucy wasn't sure how long she sat on the porch after Jake had gone. Her clothes were still damp from the night before and she reached for the mug to warm herself but the coffee was cold and cloudy on top and she dumped it over the rail. She waited awhile but the chill seemed to wrap around her and she got up slowly and went inside, thinking vaguely about fixing some more coffee. The sink in the kitchen was crowded with mugs and plates, an empty pizza box, a flyswatter, a pair of chopsticks. She found a jar of instant coffee and started to pick up the kettle from the back of the stove but suddenly a terrible thick tiredness washed over her and she closed her eyes and rested her head against a cupboard door. After a few minutes she pushed herself away from the sink and went through the living room to the bedroom in back, where she fell in a heap on the unmade bad, pulling a blanket up off the floor and bundling it around her.

The numbers on the clock said 12:03 when Lucy opened her eyes and for a while she lay staring at them, watching as they blinked forward to 12:04, 12:05, 12:06. Moving carefully, she rolled onto her back as she tried to remember where she was and why she was there. The wind caught the curtains and blew them into the room, the air chilled her, and it all came back: the rain, the thunder, the boy named Jake. "And me throwing up on the beach," she said out loud.

She got out of bed and stood there looking around the room. The floor was heaped with clothes and the closet door was open and off the track. Over the bed there was a poster of a movie called *The Last Wave* and on the wall opposite there was another, this time of a mountain that rose majestically in black and white, soaring, or so it seemed to Lucy, up into the shadows of the room, through the ceiling and beyond. She moved over to the dresser, running her fingers along a pair of sunglasses, a broken conch shell, a paperback book. The mirror was stuck all round with snapshots, and Lucy leaned close to look at the people, who all seemed to be smiling at her. People in back yards and on the beach, at someone's birthday party, in front of a Christmas tree.

She took a picture from the bedside table and carried it into the living room, holding it up to the light and looking at Jake, in a cap and gown, surrounded by what had to be his family. "Make yourself at home," she heard him say again and she put the picture on top of a stereo speaker and watched him watch her as she moved around the room. The couch was low and had a sprung look and in front of it was a footlocker jumbled over with books and tapes, an empty coffee mug. Lucy read the book titles out loud, "*The Great Gatsby, Our Town, The Old Man and the Sea,*" holding them up to her nose and breathing in the damp musty smell. She sorted through a pile of paperbacks by someone named Adrian Blair, feeling the worn softness of their covers, and examined the tapes scattered across the trunk. She sat in a tumbledown rocking chair, letting her head fall back and looking up at the faces of a man and a woman who stared back at her from out of carved wood frames. The photographs were in shades of brown and water-stained around the edges. The man was thick and stern, with a heavy mustache, while the woman seemed to be all lines and angles, with her hair pulled back, her ears sticking out on either side of her head.

"Quit your looking at me," said Lucy, jumping up and letting the chair rock back against the wall. "Quit looking at me like I'm something that the tide dragged in."

But from over the couch the man and woman continued to stare out at her.

She climbed up onto the couch, lifting first the man and then the woman off the wall, staggering under the weight of them. "I don't want you watching me," she said, leaning close to the woman and talking to her, nose to nose. But just then the glass caught her own reflection and held it for a minute, so that she found herself studying her white pointed face, her sunken eyes, her hair matted against her head.

Lucy propped the picture against the wall and went in search of the bathroom, looking at herself in the mirror, pushing her fingers through her hair, pulling at her damp and draggled dress. She yanked off her clothes and let them fall in a pile on the floor. She ran her fingers down her body, holding them at her waist before she turned on the shower full force and stepped under it. "Vanity of vanities; all is vanity." The words rose up from out of her childhood and bounced off the tiles. "Vanity of vanities," she heard her father's voice. "No," she shouted. "No." She scrubbed her hair, her body, and turned to face into the stream of water. When she got out, she reached for a towel and rubbed her skin until it burned. She pinched her cheeks and looked in the mirror again.

"That's some better," she said.

"Vanity of vanities," the tiles whispered.

"That's a lot better," she said as she grabbed a brush off the shelf and attacked her hair.

Wrapped in a towel, Lucy went to the door and looked out to make sure there was no one in sight before darting onto the porch. She found her bag and carried it inside, upending it on the kitchen table. The clothes were wet and had a sour smell and she left them there and headed for the bedroom. She poked at the piles of Jake's clothes on the floor and finally found a pair of sweatpants, a sweatshirt, and put them on, feeling suddenly warm and safe.

"I ought to eat something," she said. But the words were scarcely out of her mouth before she had climbed up on the bed and was back asleep.

Six

"What happened to Hector and Presilla?" the voice asked, pushing its way through walls of sleep. And for a minute Lucy thought it belonged to Liddy, that her sister was talking her awake, the way she had done so many times in the past. Or Mama, maybe. Or Doris or Warren.

"I found them face to the wall as though they'd done something they shouldn't've," the voice went on, but this time Lucy could tell that it was deep and rumbly and crinkled around the edges with the sound of laughter that had either just stopped or was waiting to begin. She opened her eyes and saw Jake sitting at the foot of the bed, looking down at the pictures of the man and woman that were now propped against the dresser.

"They're doing it again," said Lucy, moving quickly to the head of the bed, crouching back into the corner.

"Doing what?" said Jake.

"Looking at me. They were doing it before. In the front room. Looking at me like I wasn't meant to be here. Like I was something the tide carried in. The way my pa looks at people some."

"How's that?"

"Oh, I don't know. Leave it be." Lucy jumped off the bed and went into the kitchen and stood at the table, pawing through her still-damp clothes, shoving them back into her bag.

"Don't," said Jake, coming in behind her. "They've got to be wet, after last night, and they'll mildew and grow fuzz and you'll smell like the underside of a rock."

"I took a shower," said Lucy.

"I didn't say you *did*, I said you *will*—if you wear mildewed clothes. Here, let's spread them out so they can dry." He reached for a skirt, a couple of blouses, a jacket, and draped them over the chairs, then grabbed a handful of underwear and headed for the bathroom.

"No," called Lucy, running after him.

"Yes," said Jake, hanging bras and underpants along the shower rod. "What's the big deal, I know about gir-rr-llls. Anyway, I have a sister, and a mother. And besides that, I was taken to museums at an early age and they all had *naked* statues."

Lucy looked back at her clothes strung along the rod and felt her face grow warm. "Clothe your nakedness, Lucy Peale," she whispered just under her breath.

"Say what?"

"Oh, nothing. It's just something somebody said once."

"Your father?"

"Somebody." And she pushed her way past him and went back to the living room, trying to think of what to talk about next. "Tell me about them," she said, pointing to the empty wall over the couch. "About Hector and Presilla. Are they kinfolks?"

"Not of mine, they're not. But they must've been someone's, along the line. That's the point. Why I rescued them from the trash barrel. I mean, they've obviously had a past."

"But you knew their names?"

"Nope. No way *of* knowing. No spidery writing on the back in faded brown ink that says 'William, Ethel.' Not even a 'Mother, Father.' That's why I had to take them on."

Lucy sat down on the couch and twisted to look up at the wall in back of her. "I don't understand. You've got a man and a lady hanging on your wall—"

"They *were* hanging there. You took them down, remember?"

"You've got a man and a lady with no-account names—"

"Hector and Presilla aren't 'no-account' names, they're perfectly *good* names," said Jake. "I put a lot of thought into those names. I looked at their faces and knew right off they weren't John and Mary, or Horace and Esmeralda. I read the phone book and the death notices and my sister's name-the-baby book and came up with names that fit like a name is meant to fit. Same as in the stories I write."

"You write stories?" said Lucy.

"Some," said Jake, going to stand at the screen door for a minute, then turning back to sit on a canvas chair slung low to the ground. "Only not enough. Not as many as I thought I'd write."

"Why? Do you write them, I mean."

"Because I can't *not* write them," said Jake. And when Lucy didn't say anything, he went on. "It's a part of me— like brown eyes, or blond hair, or the scar over my eye from falling off my bike when I was seven. It started when I was a little kid and was forever telling stories to anybody who'd listen. My mother, my father, my sister, Meg. The alligator who lived in the sink."

"Alligator?" said Lucy. "A real one?"

"No." Jake shrugged. "Imagined. A made-up story for a made-up alligator. It gets weird sometimes."

"Is that why you quit school?" said Lucy. "So's you could write more stories?"

"Not really," said Jake, getting up and going to the kitchen, coming back with a bag of beer pretzels, passing one to Lucy. "The thing is, college just wasn't—God, I hate this expression and I know it turns me into a walking cliché—but it wasn't rel-e-vant anymore. A bunch of courses I thought I didn't need. The dorm. The whole bit. So I dropped out and stayed down here, waiting tables off-season, reading, walking the beach, and not writing enough. I mean, I didn't think I'd turn out the great American novel, but I figured I'd do more than this." He reached out with his foot and pointed to a spiral notebook balancing on a typewriter case under the window. "Only I'll probably go back. I'll *definitely* go back. But not this year. This year I have plans—big plans. Well, next year, actually. Starting in January."

"What kind of plans?" said Lucy.

Jake leaned over and took a book off the footlocker and held it up. "Do you know the books of Adrian Blair?"

"No," said Lucy. "I've heard of Hemingway and some of the others, from school, you know. But not him."

"Yeah, he's not all that well known here, until recently. He's English, lives in London, but he's coming to Maryland, to Baltimore, to Hopkins—and I've got a job working for him."

"What kind of job?" asked Lucy, thinking that the pretzels were making her hungrier than she had been before.

"As a dogsbody."

"Dogs—what?"

"Dogsbody. It's a sort of a drudge, a body slave, a kind of general factotum."

"Why'd you want to be that?"

"Because it's for Adrian Blair, *with* him, and I'll get to talk to him, and learn from him, about writing and books. And besides being a chance of a lifetime, there's a certain satisfaction in at least theoretically telling the university to stick it in their ear."

"How come?" said Lucy.

"It's a long story, sort of," said Jake. He waited for a minute and when Lucy didn't say anything he went on. "When I heard that Adrian Blair was coming as writer-in-residence to Hopkins, I asked about taking his courses, only to be told that they were *graduate* courses and not for the likes of me, or any other dropout. So I went straight to the source."

"Huh?" said Lucy, putting her head back on the couch and thinking that she was still sleepy.

"I wrote to Adrian Blair in England, explaining the situation and asking if he could help."

"And could he?"

"No. He wrote back that he couldn't interfere with the workings of Academe but that if I was interested in a job as dogsbody—that he was confined to a wheelchair now and needed help, a driver, somebody to be on call more or less, live in the house they've rented for him. Be a—"

"Dogsbody," said Lucy.

"Yes. And that's what makes it such a plum. Because he *is* so disabled, and getting older, he's not likely to do this again. At least not in the States. But enough of that. Now, how about you? Where're you in school? What year?"

"I'm done and I'm never going back," said Lucy, licking the salt off her pretzel. "School wasn't ever something I was much in favor of, maybe because of the way Pa always made us come home right at three o'clock and not go to things afterwards, you know. So when I graduated from high school this year, Doris and I took our notes and papers and folders and burned them in a big old metal trash can out by the back door. Ma like to had a fit. Thought we were going to burn the whole place down. Tent and all."

"Tent?"

"Yeah, it's where Pa has his church," said Lucy, locking her arms across her chest.

Jake shrugged and said, "Who's Doris, then?"

"My sister. My favorite sister. She's a year older than me but we finished up at the same time on account of back in fifth grade Miss Woods thought I was right smart at catching on to things and shoved me up ahead of myself and I just stayed there."

"So," said Jake. "School's out and you've burned your bridges and your books. Now what?"

"I didn't burn any books, or any bridges either. I never would. Just papers and such."

"It's an expression. A figure of speech. Do you like books?"

"I like 'em some," said Lucy. "We didn't have all that many at home. Just the Bible and a couple of others, and the magazines that came in for Pa, with preachy sayings done up in fancy writing. But I used to like the books at school. The reading ones, not the textbooks. And just the other day, when I was up to the library, I was thinking how I could maybe stay there forever."

"Is that what your father is? A clergyman?"

"You're doing it again. Like you were last night. Asking too many questions. Go on and tell me about Hector and Presilla and how you came to save them from the trash barrel."

Jake got up and went to put a tape on, waiting for the music to begin before saying, "Louis Armstrong. Do you like jazz?"

"I might," said Lucy, putting her head back against the couch and feeling the rhythm, listening to the wail of a horn.

They sat for a few minutes without speaking before Jake went on. "My mother has this store, see. A secondhand shop. Well, it's more than that. She specializes in Victoriana. Oddments and collectibles. A lot of stuff: fans and brooches and dishes so ugly you almost have to like them; old sheet music and doorsteps and dolls with china heads.

Anyway, she's forever going off to house sales, estate sales, and coming home with what she can find. That's how she came across Hector and Presilla—but she just wanted the frames and was ready to scrap the pictures. Only by then I'd latched on to them, named them and all, so I talked her into hanging them in the store 'as is,' and when nobody bought them—I think she overpriced them on purpose, 'cause by then they were part of the family almost—anyway, when nobody bought them and I decided to stay here year round, she brought them down to me." He looked for a minute at the empty spaces over the couch. "Now, shall we put them back, where they belong?"

"I still don't like them," said Lucy when Jake had gone to the other room and come back carrying the pictures. "I don't like the way they're looking straight out in front all hard-eyed like they're seeing nothing and everything both at the same time."

"That's because of the times, and the way people posed when they were getting their pictures taken then," said Jake. "But think of them later, or before, in real life. Think of them alone together. Or looking at each other over the children's heads. During supper or at church on Sunday."

"Children? Hector and Presilla had children?" said Lucy, getting caught up in the story in spite of herself.

"Six," said Jake.

"*Six?* Are you sure?"

"Six. And *she* read them stories and *he* made a wagon out of wood for them to play with. And they both looked under the beds and behind the clothes in the wardrobe when the kids were scared at night."

"Hector and Presilla did *that*?" said Lucy, reaching out tentatively and touching the glass that covered the faces. "And they might maybe've had a cat, I reckon," she said after a while.

"A cat? You're right. Why didn't I think of that." And Jake jumped up and went to rummage in the closet. He came back carrying a flat square package and stood tearing off the brown paper as he spoke. "I got this up on the boardwalk one night. The artist was selling them, there was a whole series, and he wasn't doing well and it was late and he kept reducing his prices, so I just stood there waiting, and I finally got this for $5." He held up a watercolor of a fat white cat with red pouchy cheeks looking out from behind a bowl of blue-and-pink flowers. "He's a caricature, almost. The way that Hector and Presilla are caricatures, except they're not. And he's a worthy cat for the two of them." He taped the watercolor on the wall over the couch and hung Hector and Presilla back on their hooks so that they flanked it on either side and the three of them stared out into the room. The man, the woman, and the fat white cat.

"I'm starved," said Jake. "D'you find anything here to eat today?"

"I didn't even look, because I mostly slept. Except for waking up the once to take a shower and put this on," she said, plucking at the gray sweatsuit. "I'm gonna wash it, though. And put it back."

"Hey, no big deal." He got up, went to the kitchen, and threw open the door to the refrigerator. "Yeah, look at this. Dead pizza, half a carton of OJ, and beer." He put the juice and a plate with two slices of pizza on the table and said, "Forget this. I'll get carryout. What d'you feel like eating? Subs? Chinese? Or we could go somewhere. A bunch of the guys are getting together at the Smorg. We do that a lot, especially after a storm, to talk about the pulls, the near misses, to kind of cheer each other up."

"No," said Lucy, coming to stand by the kitchen table. "I can't, but you—"

"It's not just guys. There're girls, too."

"I still can't," said Lucy. "But you go on. Besides, I'm leaving here."

"Leaving for where? You going home?"

"I can't go home."

"Where, then? Back to the boardwalk—*under* the boardwalk?"

"The storm's over. And it's just for one night," said Lucy, "because I'm getting a job tomorrow."

"Yeah, but even so, they don't pay in advance around here and any halfway decent place you can find to live'll want some money up front." He leaned back against the refrigerator and watched her for a minute. "Look, why don't you just figure on staying here till you find a job and actually get paid. There's room."

"And what do you want?" said Lucy, suddenly feeling the faceless Phil crowding around her.

"Give me a break," said Jake, slamming his hand down on the top of the refrigerator. "I thought we settled this last night—how I'm not Mel Gibson, but I'm not King Kong either. There's the bed *and* the sofa bed, take your pick. Meanwhile, I'll keep a running tab, okay? Rent.

Food. Hot water. Use of the sweatsuit. Now tell me, are subs okay?"

"We could eat this," said Lucy, pointing to the food on the table. "And if you have any tea bags, any crackers . . ."

"*This?*" said Jake. "The pizza's turned to plastic and the OJ's of indeterminate age. It may even have fermented by now, if orange juice does that. But the beer's okay. That's the thing about beer—nothing happens to it. Anyway, I'm out of here. But I'll be back bearing food."

After Jake had left, Lucy ate the two pieces of pizza, scraping the hard cold cheese off the plate and licking her fingers when she was done. She took the plate over to the sink and stood for a minute looking down at the clutter that was there before she picked up the old pizza box, folded it in half, and stuffed it down into the trash can. Turning on the water full-force, she washed the dishes and put them on the drainboard, hanging the flyswatter on a hook and lining the chopsticks along the windowsill.

Out on the porch, the little table still lay in a heap from the night before. Lucy picked it up, fitting the legs back in place, setting it between the chairs. She looked over the rail and saw the "Summer Wind" sign dangling. She went down the steps and was trying to hook it back on the pole when Jake pulled up in a green Toyota. "Hey, you don't have to mess with that. It needs a screw and I'll fix it later. Meanwhile, starvation's setting in. Come on, Lucia," he called over his shoulder as he took the steps two at a time.

"Roast beef," he said, taking subs out of the bag. "And roast beef. That way there's no discussion. No decisions to be made. But if you're a vegetarian I'll trade my tomatoes for your beef. My lettuce, too, if you drive a hard bargain."

"No," said Lucy. "That's fine. Except I ate the pizza already."

"Count it as an appetizer, then. The finest meals always have appetizers." He reached in the bag and took out another carton of orange juice and one of milk and set them on the table. "There're napkins under the sink and plates in the cupboard."

While they ate, Jake talked about the storm and how it had just about blown itself out to sea, about how tomorrow would be fair. He talked about the Beach Patrol and what it was like to be a lifeguard, about riptides, and the things people say or don't say after they've been pulled in. "A lot of them are embarrassed," said Jake. "Especially the macho types. They go off, half the time in a huff, trying to pretend it never happened." He rolled the sub papers into a ball and dropped it into the trash when he got up to get a beer. "Okay, no fair. I've done all the talking. Now it's your turn. What kind of a job do you want to get?"

"I don't know. Anything. I can't do much."

"Hey, look, you don't have to be a rocket scientist to do most of the scut work down here. There're restaurants and stores and beach stands. There're malls and about a thousand and one Ma-and-Pa operations—all looking for slave labor. And, now that it's the middle of August, kids are bailing out right and left, so take your pick and tomorrow we'll see what we can find."

"It makes no never-mind," said Lucy, getting up to take a glass out of the cupboard. Then, remembering how the smell of food up on the boardwalk had made her sick, she added, "Maybe in a store, then. Someplace that sells something, not to do with food." She pushed the glass across the table to Jake. "Can I have some of that beer? I never did before, I even told somebody once that it smelled like baby throw-up, but I'm thirsty and milk is—" She stopped and wrinkled her nose and made a face.

Jake pulled the can out of reach. "I don't think so. You'd better not," he said. "I remember from my sister that beer's not—that you're not supposed to have it. I mean, if there's a baby and all."

"No," said Lucy, jumping up. "Who said anything about a baby. Who said I had a baby in me." She flattened her hands against her stomach. "Besides, you can't tell from hardly," she said as she ran out of the apartment and onto the porch.

Jake followed her outside and stood with his arms around a post, looking up at the sky. In back of him, Lucy huddled in a chair, pressing her chin down against her chest. "How'd you know?" she said after a while.

"I'm not sure," said Jake, turning to sit on the porch rail. "I just thought it. My sister has three kids and I remember what it was like for her in the beginning—puking her guts up—"

"I didn't," said Lucy. "I was a little sick, is all."

"And something about your eyes. That sort of shadowed look. All Meg ever wanted to do was sleep, in the first three months, anyway. And there's a certain way pregnant women carry themselves, protectively, sort of, and not like later on when they look like Sherman tanks. Anyway, that's what I thought, from my limited experience." He moved to sit on a chair across from her. "But it's no—"

"Don't say it's no big deal," said Lucy, sitting forward and shaking her head.

"I wasn't going to say that," said Jake. "It *is* a big deal. It's a hell of a big deal."

"And don't tell me to get rid of it. Or to give it away, because if there is a baby it'd be mine for keeps."

"I'm not trying to tell you to get rid of it, or to give it away, either. All I'm trying to do is to keep you from drinking a beer—one lousy beer—because I know from Meg that you're not supposed to have alcohol, or caffeine, or even an aspirin. Anyway, we can talk about that later on."

"There's nothing to talk about."

"There's plenty to talk about," said Jake. "Like a doctor. Have you seen a doctor? A job. About how you'll manage the rest of your life."

The rest of your life. The words crashed down on her. They ricocheted off the porch roof, the railing, the weak-legged table, and wrapped themselves around Lucy's head, so that for a minute she was sure it would burst right open.

"No," she cried. "I can't think of that." And she was up, bumping into the little table and sending it across the porch as she headed for the steps. "I can't think of that at all."

Lucy sat on a cinder block at the edge of the parking lot behind the "Summer Wind" and looked at a purple bathing suit and a draggled beach towel hanging on a line. She watched a gull circling overhead, and the last of the clouds racing across the sky.

"Who do you think you are, Jake Jarrett?" she whispered.

"Who do you think you are?" she said again, this time out loud. "Who do you think *I* am? Another Hector? Another

Presilla? Somebody more for you to hang on your wall so's you can make a story out of 'em? I'll think of what to do with the rest of my life my own self, thank you very much. Just not tonight."

She got up and started across the parking lot, but the stones hurt her feet and she stood for a minute, rubbing first one foot and then the other. She took a deep breath and looked at the windows of Jake's apartment, thinking how she would march upstairs; how she would find her shoes, her clothes, her laundry bag; then how she would turn and leave, without saying anything at all. But when Lucy went around front she was surprised to see a pickup truck parked half on the sidewalk and to hear voices coming from the porch overhead.

She flattened herself against the side of the house and slid down the wall, pulling her legs close and staring at her bare feet. Sounds swirled around her: a word, a phrase, a bit of laughter. The light faded and the darkness settled in. An ice-cream truck came and went, its jangly tune growing fainter as it moved on to the next street over, the one after that. A dog barked. Children playing in the street were called inside.

Lucy moved closer to the corner of the building, listening for the sound of Jake's voice as it drifted down from the porch above.

Seven

The room was hot with the morning sun, and a horsefly buzzed against the window. Lucy sat up and looked around. She turned to the wall in back of her, but Hector and Presilla and the fat white cat seemed somehow preoccupied, as if they were watching something off in the distance. She rubbed her eyes and ran her fingers through her hair, thinking about the night before. She remembered how she had waited for Jake's friends to leave, for Jake to go back in and shut the door, to turn off his kitchen light, so that the little patch of ground where she sat was suddenly dark. She remembered how she had crept up the stairs and stood for a minute on the porch; how the door had been unlocked, the lamp on in the empty living room, the sofa bed pulled out.

A wave of nausea swept over Lucy and she curled onto

her side, digging her fingers into the mattress and wishing that she could stay there forever. From outside came the sound of children playing, someone throwing a ball against the side of the house. After a while she stood up, swaying for a minute before she bent to smooth the sheets, to fold the sofa bed back into itself and replace the cushions.

"No," she said as she made her way into the kitchen, rooting through her clothes piled on a chair in the corner. "No. I will not throw up. Not never again." But the bitter taste rose up in her throat and she turned and ran, dropping her clothes just inside the bathroom door and falling to her knees beside the toilet, gagging, retching, reaching up to flush and watching the vomit as it swirled around and down. She took off her sweatsuit and pulled herself up by the sink, looking in the mirror and backing away from the small, pinched face that stared back at her. She turned on the shower and stepped under it, holding on to the wall as she scrubbed at her mouth and spit into the tub.

When she was dressed, Lucy went out into the living room. Jake stood just inside the kitchen, leaning on the open refrigerator door. "I keep hoping there'll be more here in the morning than there was the night before," he said, opening the freezer compartment and pulling out the tag end of a loaf of bread. "Maybe later we'll have to go to the store and shop for real food—milk and eggs and spaghetti sauce."

Lucy put her hand up to her mouth and turned away.

"Oooops, sorry," said Jake. "I didn't mean to mention f-o-o-d. I didn't do it on purpose. How do you feel?"

She slumped onto the rocking chair and started to say that she felt fine; that if he had heard anything, it was a noise from the street, a defect in the plumbing. But her eyes were suddenly filled with tears and there was a lump in her throat and she shook her head without saying anything.

"How pregnant *are* you? How many weeks? Months?" She shook her head again.

"Do you know? I'd think that you'd know for sure," said Jake.

"I know," said Lucy, her voice flaring out into the room. "It was only the once and I *know*." She got up and headed to the porch, leaving the door open behind her and turning as soon as she got there, to come back inside. "How come you said that?" she said as Jake filled the kettle and put it on the stove. "How come you said that to me?"

"Said what?"

"That about how you thought I ought to know for sure. Like maybe I wouldn't. Like maybe there were so many. Like maybe I was a Jezebel or something."

"Jezebel," said Jake. "You? You're the least—that's the last—" He stopped, his face turning a sudden red before he went on. "Look, it's nothing to do with sex, I mean, I'd just've thought that when a girl, when it happened that there was a baby, I mean, it'd be something she'd know right off. A kind of intuition or something."

"Like magic? Like knowing something without knowing that you know it?"

"Sort of. Does that sound far out?"

"It sounds nice," said Lucy, watching as he took mugs and tea bags out of the cupboard. "Only I didn't know. On account of I didn't think this would ever happen to me. And then it was ages past, and I started getting that sick feeling in the mornings, and I counted back to my last, you know." She took the mug of tea he held out to her and carried it into the living room, waiting awhile before she said, "Two and a half months."

"Good," said Jake. "It's probably almost over then. The sickness, I mean. I know because of Meg. Because of my sister. For three months she was a case of walking death and then zap—instant cure—almost overnight she was back to being old iron-gut again. Chili, oysters, pickles. You name it."

Lucy blew on her mug and watched the tea move in ripples. I don't *care* about your sister, she wanted to say. Her and her iron gut and her pickles and her chili and her oysters, too. I'm not your sister and she's not me. I'm Lucy and I'm—

"Just ask Presilla," said Jake, pointing to the picture on the wall. "I'll bet she had morning sickness something awful."

"It's not a story," said Lucy. "Presilla's not real and I am—and it's not a story. I'm Lucy and I'm scared."

"You're right and I'm sorry," said Jake. "It's not a story. I just thought you seemed so—if you could just . . ." He shrugged and held a plate of toast out to her, the pieces curled at the edges and slathered over with raspberry jam. "I found this jam in the cupboard from one of my mother's early care packages, before she figured out that there were supermarkets in Ocean City and that I knew how to use them."

"Sin City," whispered Lucy.

"Huh?" said Jake.

"Sin City."

"Not hardly," said Jake. "Not any more'n most places, I don't think."

They sat for a minute, eating toast and flicking at the crumbs with their fingers. Finally, when she had finished and licked the corners of her mouth, Lucy pointed to the picture of Presilla. "Besides," she said, "she had Hector."

"Hector Protector," said Jake.

"Hec-tor Pro-tec-tor," said Lucy, pronouncing the words slowly, then saying them over inside her head. Hec-tor-Pro-tec-tor-Hec-tor-Pro-tec-tor-Hec-tor . . .

"Yeah," said Jake after a while. "And all you have is me, Jake the Flake. Now, how about that job. I was thinking of one of the big hotels—they're open year round, the pay's not bad, and sometimes there're even tips."

Lucy stood at the window at the end of the ninth-floor hall, looking down. It was Labor Day morning, the sky was sharp and blue, even through the tinted glass, and the sunlight bounced off the ocean. She leaned her head against the pane and listened to the hotel sounds all around her: the rumble of the elevators, the squeak of a room-service trolley, the opening and closing of doors as bellhops came to pick up luggage, to take it down to the lobby. Despite the beautiful day, the beach below was strangely deserted and she remembered what Jake had said about Labor Day: when the tourists pull out and leave the town to the rest of us. To us. To me, thought Lucy. And leave Ocean City to me. She shivered slightly, thinking how Jake had promised her that tonight they would walk the boardwalk and he would show her the town the way *he* liked it. "Trust me, I'm right," he had said when she left for work this morning.

Lately Jake had been right about a lot of things. About the job here at the hotel, the hurricane that veered out to sea. About the way she felt. Lucy swallowed carefully, testing the queasiness in her stomach. That's all it was now: a little queasiness, like the feeling she got when the elevator stopped suddenly, bouncing up and then down again. So little, in fact, that most days she hardly noticed it at all. Most days she forgot about it and ate pizza and fish and cold-cut subs. And once even a soft-crab sandwich that was filled with claws and feelers and even the shell, which she crunched right through, all the while trying not to think about what she was eating.

She pushed herself away from the window, turning back to her supply cart and trundling it along to room 913. She knocked on the door, waited, and finally used her key and went inside. During her first week at the hotel, Lucy had trained under a girl named Barb, who taught her how to make the beds and put out the towels, how to arrange the little bottles of shampoo, conditioner, and body lotion on the vanity in the bathroom, and how to fold the first square of toilet paper on the roll into a triangle. "But Rule Number One is look for a tip," Barb had said. "If it's a checkout, look for a tip."

No tip, thought Lucy as she checked under the lamp on the dresser and on top of the television set. No tip, but at least the room's not a mess. Not like some. She changed the sheets on the beds, gathered the towels from the bathroom, and scoured the tub and sink and toilet. She dusted and vacuumed and put fresh writing paper in the desk drawer. She picked up the window cleaner and sprayed the full-length mirror, rubbing at the misted glass and watching herself emerge. For a minute she stood tugging at her rose-colored uniform before she turned sideways, rested her hands on her stomach, and tried to see if there was a bulge. "You can hardly tell, not yet anyhow," she said to the girl in the mirror, suddenly not sure whether she was glad or sorry. Then she arched her back and thrust her belly forward, trying to see what she would look like next month, or the one after that, or the one after *that*.

Before moving to another room, Lucy went out on the little balcony, holding tight to the railing and looking down at the water. From this high up, the ocean seemed flat and calm, and she tried to picture herself jumping up and down in it; tried to picture herself actually swimming. "And I could, I almost could," she said out loud, speaking into the breeze. "Except for Pa."

She went inside and stood in front of the mirror again, pulling her skirt up high over her knees, remembering Jake's reaction when he found out she had never owned a bathing suit.

"Never owned a *bathing suit?*" he had said. "*Everybody's* got a bathing suit. My *grandmother's* got a bathing suit. And my *Aunt Florence. Hector* and *Presilla* had bathing suits. What's the big deal? How'd you swim, then?"

"I never did," said Lucy. "Not me or Doris or Liddy either one. Except for once we squirted each other with the hose but with our clothes on. That's on account of Pa saying there was sin in nakedness."

"Nakedness? Who's talking about nakedness?" Jake had

said as he slapped his forehead and rolled his eyes. "We're not into nude swimming here in Ocean City. Fact is, you've got to search some to find a thong, or even a string bikini."

"Pa says—"

"I don't care what Pa says," said Jake. Lucy gasped and put out her hand as if to stop him, but he went on anyway. "Everybody's got to have a bathing suit. Especially if they're living here, with the ocean and the beach and the sun. It's unnatural not to. Un-American. Unreal. And I'm gonna get you one."

And Jake had come home a few days later with a yellow bathing suit stuffed in a paper bag. "I know these girls up on Thirteenth Street—Pam and Chrissie and Meaghan. You've met them, Chrissie goes with T.J., you know, the guard at the next station down. Anyway, people're forever moving in and out of their place and half the time they leave things behind—hair dryers, beach towels, clothes. Once even a chair. So I went by to see what they could come up with and found this suit. It's not new, but it's okay. And I think it'll fit," he had said.

While Jake was asleep that night, Lucy had gone into the bathroom and taken off all her clothes and tried the suit on. She stood on the edge of the tub peering at herself in the mirror, but her arms and legs seemed pale and splotchy and she felt suddenly chilled, as if she were caught in a draft. After that, whenever Lucy went to the beach, she wore her regular clothes, sitting on the sand with her arms around her knees. And when Jake asked about the bathing suit she said, "Next time," or "Later," or "Not today."

"But yes—today," said Lucy, closing the curtains and

giving the room a final check. "Today I'm going to the beach in my first ever bathing suit, on account of most of the tourists heading home and leaving the town to me and Jake." She picked up the vacuum cleaner and went out into the hall.

Lucy walked along the beach in her yellow bathing suit with one of Jake's T-shirts over the top and a beach towel wound around her waist. She kept her head down, concentrating on the sand in front of her and looking back, from time to time, to the string of footprints stretching behind her. "There's sin in nakedness, Lucy Peale"—the words seemed to pulse around her, caught in the cry of a gull and the breaking of a wave, in the rumble of the boardwalk train. I'm not naked, thought Lucy, pulling at her T-shirt and clutching the towel. I've got me a bathing suit on and I'm not naked one little bit. She thrust her head forward and walked faster, moving out to kick her feet at the shallow water and then back to dry sand.

"Hey, lady, watch the castle."

Lucy stopped and stepped back, looking down at the tumbled heap of sand. A little boy stood in front of her, his feet apart, his hands on his hips. "You got the tower," he said. "And it was the best one, the one they were going to put the bad guys in."

"Oh," said Lucy, dropping down on her knees and pushing at the wet sand. "I'm sorry. I could try and fix it."

"You need a bucket, and a stick or something to make the going-down places," the boy said, and he turned and went a little ways up the beach, coming back with a pail and shovel, and followed by three little girls. The children

87

squatted in a circle around Lucy, watching as she scooped wet sand into the bucket and turned it carefully, tapping on the bottom before she lifted it off.

"I'm Andrew," the boy said after a while. "And that's my sister, Maggie. And they're my cousins, Katie and Pilar. What's your name?"

"I'm Lucy," said Lucy, concentrating on repairing a part of the moat.

"You're a good tower maker," said Andrew, and Lucy felt a smile slide across her face. "And now you can swim with us," the little boy went on.

"Oh, Andrew, don't," said a woman who came to stand behind the children. "Maybe your new friend has someplace to go. Maybe she's on her way to somewhere."

"She's not," said Maggie, holding out her hand to Lucy.

"Are you?" said Andrew.

"Yes," said Lucy, "but I can go there in a spell, same as now."

"Where?" said Katie. "Go where?"

"To meet a friend. He's a lifeguard on Fifteenth Street and I was on my way up there."

"But first she'll swim with us," said Andrew, getting up and heading down to the water's edge.

"I don't know—I mean—it's just that—I never—" said Lucy, the words tumbling down around her.

"Oh, they don't really *swim*," the woman said. "They can only go in this sort of pond between the sandbar and the shore, but they *think* it's swimming. Don't let them trap you, though. Don't feel you *have* to."

But by then Maggie was tugging at one of Lucy's hands

and Pilar at the other, with Andrew and Katie dancing out in front.

"I'm a sea monster," said Andrew, flopping down on his stomach. "And you guys got to sit there and let me catch you." The girls sat in the water and Lucy sat with them. They lay on their backs, propped up on their elbows, and let the water wash over them. And Lucy lay next to them. They rolled on their sides and made sea-monster noises. They pretended they were whales and sharks and snapping turtles. And so did Lucy.

"Your towel," screeched Pilar, jumping up and pulling at Lucy's towel, dragging it up to the shore, and dropping it in a sodden heap on the sand. "It's all wet."

"That's no never-mind," said Lucy, scooping water in her hands and holding it against her face.

When it was time for the children to leave, Lucy stayed on for a minute in the pool by herself, looking at where they had been and thinking that suddenly the ocean didn't seem as big as it had before. Then she got up and wrung out her towel before she went on up the beach.

Jake was just coming down off the lifeguard stand when Lucy got to Fifteenth Street. "Well, look at you," he said when he saw her. "You've been swimming." He reached up and brushed a smudge of sand off her face.

"Not swimming for real," said Lucy, "but I was a sea monster and a snapping turtle."

"You look like a little kid."

"Don't you make fun of me, Jake Jarrett."

"I'm not making fun, Lucia," said Jake. "It's just that you look—you look the way I think you're meant to look."

Lucy stood still for a minute, feeling the closeness of him all around her. Then she turned and started away, stopping after a minute and waiting for him to catch up with her. And Jake took her hand and led her out to meet a wave rolling gently in.

Lucy and Jake ate dinner with Chrissie and T.J. at the Captain's Cove. "Let's go heavy on the tip," said Jake as they divided up the check.

"Right, we know," said Chrissie.

"Yeah," said T.J.

"To celebrate the end of summer," they all chanted in unison.

"I really love Labor Day night," said T.J. when they were outside, standing on the corner. "Look—no traffic jams. No lines for miniature golf. No sirens." They turned and walked the block to the boardwalk, stopping at the top of the ramp and looking out at the dark ocean.

"We can even walk together," said Chrissie. "And not have to go single file, snaking in and out." They turned and headed south, going past small frame hotels where the porches were lined with empty rocking chairs, past the ice-cream parlor, where only a handful of people sat at the tables out front.

"It doesn't last, you know. Not like this, anyway," said Chrissie, leaning toward Lucy. "I mean, the tourists come back for weekends, sometimes longer, through the end of October. And up where you work, they're here year round. But not like summer."

"Yeah," said Jake. "And soon a lot of these places'll be boarded up. That's when we can really go native."

"Peace. It's heaven, don't you think, Lucy?" said T.J., throwing his arms up over his head.

And Lucy nodded, walking with the three of them and feeling warm in spite of the wind, and suddenly safe.

"Well, nothing's perfect. Look up there," said Jake when they had gone a little farther. He stopped and pointed to a crowd gathered under the light at Division Street.

"What is it?" said Lucy.

"People like us, I guess, out to reclaim the boardwalk."

"No, I mean, what are they looking at?"

"I don't know," said Jake. "Maybe the sand sculptor, or somebody selling something."

"No," said T.J. "I know. It's probably that same character who was here last night." He swung around to face them, walking backward and pulling at his collar, making his eyes go wide and wild. "Hey, sinner," called T.J. "That's what he says. I mean, you can just be walking by and this clown yells out, 'Hey, sinner.' Come on, you got to see this. This guy's a kick." And he led them over toward the beach, pointing out white placards in the shape of tombstones set in the sand with sayings written on them.

"They're all about sin and damnation, with a Hallelujah thrown in from time to time," said Chrissie, pushing to get close to the front. "Come on."

Lucy hung back, afraid of what she would find if she followed Chrissie through the crowd. She pulled at Jake's sleeve. "Let's get out of here."

"No, wait," he said. "I want to see this."

Then the voice rose up. "Hallelujah and Praise the Lord, all you sinners. I'm here tonight because you didn't come to me. You didn't see fit to come on out to the Church of the Saving Grace. Not you, or you, or any one of you. So I've come here: to Sin City: to the Devil's playground. And I've come to talk about pleasure palaces and sin. About nakedness and degradation."

"No." The cry rose in Lucy's throat and hung there, barely audible, before it was caught in the wind and twisted away. She saw, as if in slow motion, Jake turn, and without waiting for him to speak she ran, not stopping until she reached the apartment.

Lucy heard Jake on the stairs outside. She thought about getting up, moving to another room, but there was noplace to hide, and instead she put her face on the back of the couch, feeling the vinyl cold against her forehead. He came in the door and across the room, sweeping the books and tapes off the footlocker and sitting on it, leaning close to her.

"Lucy—" When she didn't answer, he reached out and touched her on the shoulder.

"Leave me be," she said, rearing up as if to run. "Just leave me be."

"No," said Jake, pulling his hand away but otherwise not moving. "I'm not going to leave you be and for once you're not going to beat it out of here. For once you're not taking off through the door and down the steps. I want to talk. I want *you* to talk."

"About what?"

"About that man up on the boardwalk."

"What about him?"

"How maybe he's just some weirdo preacher who, for

some reason, scared you half to death. Or—how maybe he's your father."

Lucy burrowed deeper into the couch, shaking with the cold that only she could feel. Jake watched her for a minute, then went to get a blanket from the closet, draping it over her and tucking it around her.

"It didn't take much to figure it out," he said. "What with all that talk about Sin City and nakedness. And from the look on your face. Want to talk about it? About him?"

"I can't," said Lucy, looking up. "Anyways, you're too close."

Jake got up and moved across the room to the rocking chair. And for a while they sat with the silence thick between them until Lucy thought she would be swallowed up by it.

Her voice, when she finally spoke, was small and quick. "It's just that Pa brought us in to town—me and Doris— to hand out flyers for the Church of the Saving Grace and it was so beautiful. Ocean City, I mean. Just the way I thought it'd be when I used to see it from across the bay. All sparkly, with the lights and the music. And there were these fellas and they talked to us and the next night they took us on rides and then came out the road, to where we lived, and they—they brought—they gave us—and then afterwards—this one, he took me down to his car—and he—he—" She wiped the tears from her face without turning away. "I didn't want him to do what he did."

"But *he* did that to you, Lucy," said Jake, his voice catching on the words. "You know that, don't you?"

"Ye-es," said Lucy. "I know it deep down, but sometimes

I have to keep saying it over. Telling myself it again and again. And then when Pa found out—about the, you know."

"The baby?"

"When Pa found out, then he said as how I had to come forward at the meeting that very night and tell my sin for everybody to hear and how if I didn't then I was no kin of his and how there was no place for me in his house. And I couldn't do it. Didn't want to do it. That'd be like saying I was what he said I was—a Jezebel and a—that my baby was bad, too, and I know it's not. Same as I know I'm not." She folded her arms across her stomach and rocked back and forth.

"What about your mother? Couldn't she—"

Lucy shook her head. "Not against Pa."

"And so you left? And came to Ocean City?" said Jake.

"And I'm not going back. I can't go back. Besides, I don't want to be any kin of his, or live in his house—either one." She sat for a while without saying anything and then went on, speaking softly, as if to herself. "It's strange, and I never thought it'd happen, but I talk to God some lately, about what happened and how maybe if I'd been strong enough I could've kept it from happening, about taking care of me and my baby. About taking care of me so's I can take care of my baby. But the God I talk to isn't like Pa's. He's—he's—"

" '. . . a God ready to pardon, gracious and merciful, slow to anger, and of great kindness,' " said Jake.

"What's that?" said Lucy. "Where'd it come from?"

"I don't know," said Jake, leaning back and looking at the ceiling, then sitting suddenly forward. "Yes, I do. From

94

Sunday school, on a sign over the blackboard, with clouds on it, and a sort of beam of light."

"What?" said Lucy.

"We went to Sunday school—Meg and I—while our parents went to church on Sundays, and this one year I had Mrs. Taylor for my teacher." He stopped and made a face. "I remember it now. She had a wart, with a hair growing out of it, and a voice like broken glass, so when she talked I didn't listen but instead I memorized all the things in the classroom. You know, the books of the Bible, prayers, little sayings. I thought I'd forgotten all that stuff."

"Tell me it again," said Lucy.

" 'Thou art a God ready to pardon, gracious and merciful, slow to anger, and of great kindness.' "

Eight

The baby moved. It was near about the middle of October, a Tuesday night, and I was home in the apartment alone. Jake was waiting tables up at the Pier and I wasn't doing much of anything except listening to a tape till it was time to go to the movies with Chrissie. We did that some, hung out together, when Jake and T.J. were both working. And it was nice. Sort of like having Doris back again, but not quite, on account of Chrissie and I mostly talked around the edges of things and not really *about* anything the way my sister and I used to do. Mostly I think that was because of the baby and Chrissie not knowing what to say. Jake let on as how he had told T.J. and we both figured *he'd* told *her*. Besides, it was nice having somebody to do stuff with and she went with me once to get my hair cut and taught me how to use blush so's I wasn't always having to pinch hard at my cheeks to make them red and shiny.

But, anyway, about the baby. I felt it. At least I thought I did. Something small and fluttery like maybe a butterfly deep inside of me. And the first thing I did was go to the phone and call Chrissie and tell her I couldn't go. My voice must've sounded funny, 'cause for a while there she kept asking, "Is anything wrong? Is everything all right? Shall I come over?"

I thought quick and said, "I have a sore throat, and maybe a cold coming on. Could we go tomorrow?"

And Chrissie said, "Sure. No big deal. I'll call you then."

After that, I just turned off the tape and lay flat on the floor to wait, with old Hector and Presilla looking down at me. For a while there, nothing happened, except for someone slamming a door in the next apartment and the wind whistling around the corner of the building, the way it does when it's coming from the north. I waited, and I waited, and *still* nothing happened. I pushed my hand down inside my pants, flat against my stomach, and closed my eyes. And then I felt it. The same small butterfly feeling.

And I knew. I knew. I sat bolt upright and wrapped my arms around my knees and hugged them close. When I looked over at the pictures of Hector and Presilla, for a minute I was sure I saw Presillla's mouth twitch into a teeny tiny smile, like we knew a secret together. Just the two of us.

And for a while there, I felt that I was going to pop. That the room was too small to hold me. I went outside, to the porch, and stood looking up at the stars, and I was laughing and crying both at the same time, on account of now I knew for sure that the baby was real. More real than it'd ever been before. I wanted to say something to it but I felt right simple. Then I didn't care and I leaned down as close as I could get to my belly and I whispered, "Okay. It's okay. And you're gonna be—what is it Jake says his mother says—you're gonna be safe as pockets."

After that, I went inside, got washed, pulled out the sofa bed, and climbed in. Most nights, when Jake's working late, I stay up, sort of dozing on the couch, so's when he comes in we can have something to eat, or a cup of cranberry tea together. But not that night. That night I just wanted to go off by myself. Me alone, and the baby. To think about things.

I didn't have to work the next day, so I slept till after ten. When I awoke, Jake was at the kitchen table drinking coffee, and I pushed myself up on my elbow and said, "The baby moved," right out, hardly even remembering how I was going to keep it a secret. For a while, anyway.

"The baby moved?" shouted Jake. And he was up and around the room. Marching, sort of, over the top of the sofa bed and down again, flicking a dish towel, looking up at Hector and Presilla and saying, "The baby moved.

"Why didn't you tell me?" he said. "Why didn't you wait up, or leave a note?" And just looking at his face I could tell how he really wanted to know and I felt bad all over.

"I was tired," I said. "I was just going to lie here and tell you when you got home, only I fell asleep." I crossed my fingers and prayed for him to believe me.

Next thing I knew, Jake was rooting through the pile of stuff on the footlocker. "Where's that book?" he said.

"What book?" Only I knew right well, without even asking, that he was talking about the book that tells you what to expect when you're expecting that he'd brought home from the library. He found it on the windowsill and took it over to the kitchen table, flipping pages till he came to what he was after.

"It's called quickening," he said. "The baby moving for the first time."

"Quickening," I said after him, thinking how what had happened *felt* like the word *sounded*.

But Jake had already shut the book and put it back on the windowsill and was kicking at the end of the bed, the way he does sometimes when he wants me to get up.

"Quit it," I said, pushing my face down in the pillow. "It's my day off."

"Come on," he said.

"Come on where?"

"To the doctor. Today's the day. You're off from work and I don't have to go in till five. Anyway, you've stalled long enough. You should've gone *weeks* ago. Maybe even *months*. You know what the book says. And I remember from Meg."

"I don't *care* about the book. And I don't *care* about your sister, either," I said.

"You care about the baby, don't you? What's good for it?"

"Yeah, but that's not to do with you."

I heard Jake go in the kitchen and fill the kettle with water and set it on the stove. "It is, though," he said after a spell. "It's to do with me the way what happens to me is to do with you. That's how it is when people live together."

"I'll move, then," I said, sitting up and punching at the pillow, wishing for a minute that it was Jake. I found a pair of socks on the floor and put them on and pulled a sweatshirt down over my nightgown. "I'll get me a place of my own and I'll move right on out of here," I said as I got up and headed for the porch.

"Good," yelled Jake as I shut the door.

I sat on a porch chair with my feet curled under me and my clothes pulled down around me, on account of the cold, and thought how Jake and I did that a lot. Me saying I was going to move and him saying "Good." Or him saying "Nobody's forcing you to stay, you know," and me saying, "Yeah. Fine. I'll move, then." But the thing was, I was pretty sure I didn't want to move, same as I was sure Jake didn't want me to. And it wasn't only to do with the money: wasn't only because with *me* paying half the rent he could save for when he decided to go back to college, and with *him* paying half the rent I could save for the baby.

It was more than that. And I sat there looking at the houses across the street, closed up tight like folks with their eyes shut, and thinking of all the reasons Jake and I stay together. A lot of it is having someone to talk to—and who talks to me. It's having someone to leave a note for, when I go out—and who leaves a note for me. It's having someone to make tea for—and who makes tea for me. But mostly, I guess, it's the talking. A couple of times, after we saw him up on the boardwalk, I talked some more about Pa. And about Ma, too. About how even if I didn't like the things Pa said, I knew he meant them, believed in them something fierce. But not Ma. Ma just went along, being scared and lily-livered clear the way through and not at all the way I wanted to be with *my* baby. I told him about Doris, too, and how I missed her and wished I could see her. The whole time I was talking, Jake'd nod and say Uh-huh and push at me to see how I could change things. Me myself. And afterwards I always felt better than I had before.

Jake told me about his family some. About Meg and her kids and her husband, Tom. About his mother, Emma, and his father, George, who sounded the way people ought to sound. And once he even said how what he wanted someday was to have a life like his Ma and Pa's, which is maybe the nicest thing anybody can ever say.

There's other reasons, too, why Jake and I're still together. Stuff like the way we both like anchovies on pizza, and storm clouds, and yogurt-covered raisins. There's the music we listen to, and sometimes how we sing when we ride along, dumb songs, usually, like "Row, Row, Row Your Boat," and "Clementine," but once even "Amazing Grace." And how he gave me a book to read called *A Farewell to Arms* that was the saddest thing I ever read, and when I finished it, I turned back and started over before I even stopped crying. And how Jake took me to the library to get a card and walked me around, showing me his favorite books, and it was sort of like he was introducing me to people he knew. I added them all to the list in my head of books I'm going to read someday. Then I found one on my own, one Jake hadn't even read, called *A Tree Grows in Brooklyn*, about a girl named Francie, who was the toughest, realest girl I ever knew, and I read that twice over, too, and was feeling right sad about having to take it back to the library when Jake bought me a copy up at the flea market outside the Convention Center. It was old and yellow-looking, with a tattered dust jacket that had a tree on the front and a picture of Betty Smith, the lady who wrote it, on the back. And it smelled sweet and mildewy both at the same time and was the first book I ever had, just for me, and not to do with school.

I do stuff for Jake, too. I don't see how, or why it works this way, but he's told me a couple of times over that he writes more now than he did before I came to live here. Sometimes, even, in that bit of time between when I get home from the hotel and before he leaves for work up at the Pier, he reads me what he's written that day. And just listening to it, to those words from out of his head, makes me feel prickly and hot and cold all at the same time.

I sat there on that porch and thought about all this and about how Jake's been after me to go to the doctor and how I knew he was right. Except I was afraid to go. And when he asked me why, I couldn't come out and say I was plain scared to have somebody look up inside of me—afraid it would hurt—and how it'd be like somebody seeing me undressed, only worse. And what'd Pa say to that? Finally I got up and took a deep breath and went inside. "About that doctor," I said. "We probably should maybe go next week, instead."

"I already called, while you were out on the porch," said Jake. "I tried the Medical Center here in town first, and they referred us to the clinic over at the hospital in Salisbury."

"Oh, well, then. That's a ways to go, so we'll just wait a spell and—"

"It's only thirty miles," said Jake. "Besides, when I called, they said to be there by noon."

The doctor was nice. His name was Dr. Foster and he was not too short and not too tall, with hair that had just enough gray in it to let me know he'd been around awhile. I guess he could tell, without me even saying it out loud, that I was scared, 'cause he took his time and told me everything he was going to do, and why. The nurse even stood right there next to me and let me hang on to her hand for dear life. And afterwards, when he was done, Dr. Foster looked up and said, "Well, Lucy—do you mind if I call you Lucy?"

I couldn't think what else he *would* call me, so I shook my head and allowed as how it was my name and waited for him to get *on* with it.

"Well, Lucy," he started up again. "I'd say you were a very healthy young woman."

"And pregnant?" I said. I mean, I knew that I knew, but I sort of guess I wanted to hear him say it out loud.

"And pregnant," he said, coming around to the side of the table and smiling down at me and reaching out to shake my hand, like I'd done something that was maybe going to turn out all right, after all. "You get dressed now and come into my office and we'll talk," he said, turning to go out of the examining room.

We did talk. Well, mostly Dr. Foster talked and I listened. All about vitamins and what to do and what not to do, and how later I would get to see the delivery room and the nursery and stuff. And how I'd have to go to classes and learn breathing exercises and what to do to help with the birthing of the baby. And how I'd need a partner.

He looked at the paper in front of him and cleared his throat and said, "Are you married, Lucy?"

I picked at my fingernails and looked down at my stomach, shaking my head.

"Is there anyone who can help?" asked Dr. Foster. "Your mother? A sister?"

"Just Jake," I said.

"Jake?"

"He's my friend. And we live together. And he's the one who made me come here today, and got a book from out of the library about being pregnant, and won't let me drink beer or even coffee."

"Well, good for Jake," said Dr. Foster, letting out his breath with a sound like maybe he'd lost something and then found it again. "Good for Jake."

And without even knowing I was going to do it, I jumped up out of that chair, caught hold of Dr. Foster's sleeve, and pulled him out into the waiting room, dragging him over to where Jake sat next to the fish tank. 'Cause right then there didn't seem to be anything more important in this world than that the two of them should meet one another.

It wasn't till Jake and I were outside in the car that I realized what I'd done. "Oh," I said, feeling my face go hot and staring hard out the side window. "He thinks you're my baby's daddy. On account of what I said and me introducing up the two of you like that."

"I can live with it," said Jake, reaching down to squeeze my fingers for a minute before he turned on the ignition and then the radio and headed out of the parking lot. "I can live with it, Lucia."

A lot happened between my first and second doctor's appointment and the biggest thing was, I learned to drive. Jake and I went back to Salisbury one day and got me a learner's permit, and just about every day after that, soon's I got home from work, he'd take me over to Route 50 and let me practice. Out a ways and then back, stopping and starting up again, by the side of the road. And sometimes, just driving along like that, I'd feel a grin pulling across my face and a song starting up inside my head.

Another thing that happened was that we got me some maternity clothes over at the secondhand shop, and even a pair of overalls from Sears, with plenty of room for when my stomach started to grow.

And then, all of a sudden, it was November and the weather turned cold. Sharp and blue, most days, but cold, and even worse at night when we put the heat way back to save money and I piled on the blankets and stuffed my face down in the pillow. One thing I found out pretty quick about being pregnant is that you have to pee a lot. Most every night I'd wake up at least once, maybe twice, and scurry into the bathroom and then out again, hopping back in my bed and burrowing down deep.

One night, when I came out of the bathroom, I stood shivering for a minute in the hall. The door to Jake's room was ajar and I could tell, by the draft and the way the shade slapped against the sill, that he had his window open, so I went in, meaning to close it and tiptoe on back out. But instead I just waited there, letting the night air wash up around my feet and ankles and looking down at Jake. He was curled over to one side of the bed and just watching him asleep like that made me feel cold and suddenly alone. And then, without knowing I was going to do it, I eased back the covers and just slid in that bed right next to him and lay there, hardly daring to move, feeling the icy sheets get warm around me. And I listened to him breathe.

Then, all of a sudden, Jake stirred and rolled over, pushing his head down against my shoulder and moving his hand onto my stomach, my breast. "Lucy," he said in a furry voice that let me know he was still asleep. "Lucy . . . Lucy . . .

"Lucy?" And he was up and out of that bed, down at the foot, with the covers going every which way. "What are you doing here?"

I didn't answer him. I couldn't. Instead, I put my hands up and felt my face burning against my fingers.

"Lucy?"

"I got up to go to the bathroom and it was cold, so I came in to close the window, and I saw you there and I wanted for me to be there, too."

"Oh, God, Lucy, I want for you to be here, too. You can't know how much. But we can't. Not now. Not yet. This isn't the right time. There's too much . . . It's just that . . ." I watched through the shadows as Jake stood up and reached for the spread and wrapped it around him. "Come on, let's get out of here—out of this room. I'll take you back to bed."

"I'll take myself," I said. "I don't need for you to take me. Don't need for you to do anything for me, ever again." I got up and ran into the living room, turning off the light before he could get there, and diving down into my covers.

Jake sat down next to me and I kicked at him. "Don't be that way," he said. He moved to the floor, leaning against the side of the bed and looking out into the room.

"It's on account of me being fat and ugly, isn't it?" I said, hating the way I sounded and wishing I could stuff the words back in my mouth.

"You're not fat and you're not ugly," said Jake. "And I love the way you look—all sort of growing and blooming, as if you're waiting for something to happen. And until that something happens we can't—I can't—"

I felt shamed and hot, but still I wanted to say to him that people could do it, even when they were pregnant. That I'd read it in the book he'd brought from the library and then I thought how—because of Phil—I didn't think I'd want to be near anybody ever again. But this was Jake— this was different. "It's on account of it not being your baby, isn't it?" I heard myself say. "On account of—"

"It *is* my baby, Lucy. At least it will be, in every way but one. That's what I want, anyway. What I hope you want. And that day when I could tell that Dr. Foster thought I was the father I felt like standing up there and doing a soft shoe. The same way I wanted to turn to all those other women, and to the fish in the tank, and say, 'Lucy and I are having a baby.' "

He reached under the pillow and took my hand. I started to pull away but he wouldn't let me. "I want you, Lucy. You've got to know how many nights I've been in there thinking about you. I want you, but I won't sleep with you. Can't sleep with you now."

"Because I'm what Pa said? Because I'm a Jez—"

"Don't say it. Don't ever say that." And he squeezed my fingers so's they hurt.

"Right now we can't," he said, still facing away from me, out into the dark. "Right now there's too much going on in your life. There's too much stuff for you to sort through. Right now I want you here for me just the way I want to be here for you. And afterwards, if you're still— when you've really thought—then'll be time enough." He put his head forward on his knees and rocked it from side to side. "Well, not really. But it'll have to be. Because when it happens, Lucy—for us—it's got to be forever. For then and the rest of our lives."

I wanted to stay awake all through that night, to play over what Jake had said in my head, to feel his fingers against mine. But suddenly my eyes were heavy, even though the rest of me was sort of floating. I felt him lean close, felt his lips on my forehead. I heard him say, "I love you, Lucy."

Nine

Lucy ate breakfast at the McDonald's up on the highway before she went to work. She had gotten up earlier than usual, left the apartment in a hurry, and now sat at a table by the window, drinking orange juice and eating a cheese Danish, looking out at the mist that shrouded the highway. She tried to concentrate on the cold glare of the restaurant, on the tiles and the tables and the yellow plastic chairs, but still thoughts of Jake and what had happened last night crowded in around her. For a minute she tried to fight against them but then she gave up and closed her eyes, remembering the feel of his lips on her forehead, his whispered "I love you."

She shook her head and looked down at the empty tray in front of her, then went to the counter for another Danish.

"Maybe he just said that," she said to herself when she was back at the table. "Maybe he felt like he had to, on account of me throwing myself at him. On account of me climbing into bed with him." Her face flamed and she was sure that the woman at the next table could see it.

"And now I'm shamed clear through," she went on. "And I'm never going back to that apartment. Not while Jake's there, leastways. I'll dawdle some after work, go over to the mall, wait till he's gone. And I'll find me another place to live. I'll—" Lucy stood up, feeling suddenly weak at the idea of not seeing Jake. She put her trash in the container, her tray on the shelf, and went outside, crossing the street to the bus stop.

"But Jake's too—he'd never—never could—say what he meant without meaning it," she said as she peered through the fog at the headlights and the fuzzed shapes of buildings all around her. She thought of him: of the way he reached for her hand sometimes when they were driving, the way he carried whatever book he was reading in a plastic bag to keep it clean—then wrote all over the margins and stuffed it full of notes and index cards, and clippings from the newspaper. She thought of his eyes, clear and gray, and how he looked with his glasses on. She thought of his hair, the shape of his back.

The wind sang around her and she leaned into it, hearing the words "I love you, Lucy." "I love you, too, Jake Jarrett," she whispered back, wondering if she'd ever have the nerve to say it out loud. She drew a heart in the gravel in the street, then wiped it out quickly as she saw the bus bouncing toward her.

When Lucy got to the hotel, everything seemed to be

moving slowly. Because of the weather, people slept late, ordered breakfast from room service, and kept to their rooms. Lucy tried a couple of doors, but the chains were on and sleepy voices called out to her, "Come back later . . . Give us another half hour . . ." At one room a man answered wrapped in a towel and said that he had work to do and didn't want his room made up till after noon. Lucy sighed and went back to the housekeeping closet, straightening shelves and checking her cart for the second time. She moved down to the window at the end of the hall and stood looking out at the ocean, scarcely visible through the fog. She got a soda from the machine and drank it slowly as she listened to the hum of the icemaker.

Lucy waited half an hour, then another fifteen minutes, before going to the big room by the elevator, the one they usually gave to families with young children. She had it down on her list as a checkout, and when no one answered her knock she unlocked the door, pushing against it as the wind pushed back from the other side. Propping the hall door open with her cart, she ran to close the windows, fighting her way through the tangle of curtains that danced around her. She turned back into the room and caught her breath. Feathers seemed to hang in the air. Popcorn and broken pretzels littered the carpet. There were cans and bottles scattered over the dresser, the bedside table, and a cardboard bucket filled with half-eaten pieces of chicken on top of the television.

"Oh, no," said Lucy as she sank into a chair, then jumped up as she realized she was sitting on a wet towel. "It's hardly better'n a pigsty in here." She pulled out the desk chair, felt it, and sat down carefully, looking around the room and taking a mental inventory. "Something's missing," she said, letting her eyes travel slowly around the room again. They stopped at the blank wall over the couch and in a minute she was up, reaching out to feel the empty picture hook. Then she went to the phone and called for the housekeeper.

By the time Mrs. Ayres arrived, Lucy had discovered that one of the bedspreads was also gone, as well as a yellow blanket and the telephone book. "Makes you wonder, doesn't it, how some of these people live at home," the housekeeper said from the doorway. "Though, truth to tell, we haven't had a mess like this in a long time."

"What'll happen about the missing stuff?" said Lucy, suddenly worried that because the room was on *her* floor she would be responsible.

"Oh, they'll get them," said Mrs. Ayres. "First we'll make a list of what they took, of what's ruined." She picked up a split pillow and dropped it carefully into a plastic bag before more feathers could spill out into the room. "Then I'll hand my report into the office and they'll go after 'em. Maybe put it on their credit-card bill if they don't pay. Now, come on, I'll help you clean up this place."

The rest of the rooms went quickly, but even with skipping lunch, it was three o'clock by the time Lucy went down to get her coat. As she pushed the door open to the employees' locker room, she saw Jake sitting on a bench reading a book.

"What are you doing here?" said Lucy.

"Waiting for you," said Jake.

"Oh, good," said Lucy as she slumped on the bench

next to him. "I could sure use a ride home today." Then, remembering that only this morning she had decided she was too embarrassed ever to face him again, she bent over and pretended to tie her shoe.

"Well," said Jake, running his fingers through his hair and making a face. "It seemed like a good idea at the time, so I left the car home, took the bus up here, and thought that we could walk back. Together."

"Walk?" said Lucy, trying to flatten the shrillness out of her voice. "It's four miles or more. And I'm starving. I didn't take time for lunch on account of these pigs trashed one of my rooms, and anyways, I forgot to bring it from home."

"No problem," said Jake, picking a brown paper bag off the floor and holding it high. "I wasn't sure whether this'd be a late lunch, an early dinner, or afternoon tea, but here it is: peanut-butter sandwiches, bananas, and chocolate milk. Come on, we'll have a picnic."

"A picnic?" said Lucy.

"A picnic," said Jake. "You know, picnic. Have you looked outside? It's my favorite kind of beach day, for November, gray, and foggy, and sort of Gothic. But not too cold. Anyway, let's get out of here. It smells like socks."

Lucy took her jacket from her locker and followed Jake outside and around to the front of the hotel. "How about over there?" he said, pointing to a gray weathered shed that was used as a bar in summer. "We'll sit on this side, out of the wind."

When they were seated in the sand, their backs against the building, Jake unpacked the bag, piling sandwiches

113

and fruit and cartons of milk on a piece of driftwood he had spread across their laps. "There," he said. "Four of everything. Two apiece."

"I can't eat all that," said Lucy, already biting into half a sandwich. "Well, maybe I can." While they ate they talked about the weather and the gulls circling overhead, about shells and sand and the waves curling onto the shore. Whenever there was a lull in the conversation Lucy rushed to fill it, telling stories about the hotel, asking questions. "Did you get a lot of work done this morning? Is it going to rain?"

When they were finished, Jake gathered up the trash and went to find a litter basket. "Well, what do you think?" he asked, coming back. "Shall we go get the bus or do you want to walk for a while and *then* get the bus?"

"Oh, now I could walk forever," said Lucy, turning away from him and starting down the beach. "I was just tired and hungry before. That's all." They went past the hotel and the string of high-rise condominiums next to it, past empty town houses and cottages boarded against the winter. They climbed over stone jetties and kicked at sand hills. Lucy tripped over a piece of driftwood and Jake reached to steady her, keeping hold of her arm and turning her to face him.

"What is it, Lucy? You haven't looked at me since I came up here. Haven't—"

"I did, too," said Lucy. "All the time we were eating—"

"You were staring straight ahead. Or up at the sky. Or down at the sand."

"Was not."

"Were, too."

He cupped his hand under her chin and stared at her and Lucy found that she could not look away. He pulled her close, pressing her to him, and kissed her slowly, his tongue darting against hers.

"You don't know how I've wanted to do that," said Jake, stepping back, looking down at her. "Only last night, waking up like that, finding you there, I knew I couldn't trust myself. And it's too important, Lucy. It counts for too much. That's why I came up here, to make sure you understand. That you—"

And then, as if by some unspoken signal, they moved together, hanging on to each other against the wind that swirled around them. Lucy felt the same floating sensation as she had the night before when she was drifting off to sleep. But this time she was awake. She knew she was awake.

"I love you, Lucy," said Jake, whispering into her hair. "That's what matters now. And for the rest of it—we've got time. You understand, don't you?"

All of a sudden, Lucy thought she did understand: that Jake was giving her time to be sure; time to have her baby and to sort out how she felt about things; time to make up her mind. She nodded, her head against his chest, and when she spoke, her voice was small. "I understand, but I know me one thing, Jake Jarrett, and that's never going to change. I love you back something fierce." And she broke away and ran down the beach.

Jake hurried after her and caught her hand and they walked without speaking.

"I feel ten feet tall," he said after a while.

"I feel eleven," said Lucy.

"Twelve."

"Thirteen."

"Twenty-seven."

"A hundred and sixteen."

"Six hundred and four."

"A thousand."

"And maybe a million," said Jake. "A million feet tall."

They laughed and swung their hands and took giant steps on the sand.

"Let's talk about us," he said.

"And the baby?" said Lucy.

"The baby's part of us," said Jake. "Will be, anyway." They stopped and turned to each other. Jake kissed her again, this time on the tip of the nose, and Lucy threw her arms around his neck.

"I can't wait to teach it to swim," he said as they continued on down the beach. "And to ride the waves. We'll get it a ball, and a balloon . . ."

"And a pair of roller skates—on account of I always wanted roller skates," said Lucy.

"We'll read to it," said Jake. "The easy books in the beginning—*The Little House* and *Make Way for Ducklings*. Then the rest of them—*Charlotte's Web*, *Tom's Midnight Garden*, and *The Lion, the Witch and the Wardrobe*."

"And before February, starting tomorrow," said Lucy, "I'm going to get me to the library and read all those books, so's I'll know as much as the baby. And I'll save my *Tree Grows in Brooklyn* for it, too."

"We'll get a backpack," said Jake, "and take it out to see the sunrise, and the sunset, and the stars at night."

"Yeah," said Lucy, her voice sounding suddenly fretful. "But a baby'll need more'n a backpack, I reckon."

"Tell me about it," said Jake. "I have a sister who made a career out of buying baby equipment. If anybody sold it, she had it for her kids. Sometimes in duplicate."

"It'll need a crib, a car seat, a playpen . . ." said Lucy, counting things off on her fingers.

"But if it's like my nieces you can forget the playpen," said Jake.

"It'll need diapers, and booties, and some of those little sleeper things." Lucy closed her eyes and tried to remember the last baby she had seen. "Undershirts. And baby powder."

"Bluejeans," said Jake. "And a Baltimore Orioles sweatshirt."

"We'll go to the secondhand store over in Salisbury. For the big things. The crib and the—"

"Or to my sister's basement. Nobody ever throws anything away in our family. And do you know another thing this baby's going to need, Lucia?"

"No, what?"

"A room of its own," said Jake.

"But there isn't—in the apartment, I mean. Does that mean we'll need a bigger place?" said Lucy.

"And a house someday," said Jake. "With a yard, and a rake."

"A rake?"

"For leaves, in the fall."

"But there aren't hardly any leaves in Ocean City," said Lucy. "On account of it being mostly sand."

"Well, a broom, then. For the sand."

"An attic."

"And a summer vacation," said Jake.

"Where we live *is* a summer vacation," said Lucy.

"Yes, but don't you want us all to see the Grand Canyon, the Bronx Zoo, and maybe England." Jake reached for her other hand and they spun around, going faster and faster till they fell in a heap on the sand.

"And church clothes," said Lucy when she had caught her breath. "It'll need church clothes on account of I want our baby to go to church some. On account of I want for it to know about God—but not Pa's kind of God, with the shouting and the sin worse'n anything. And all the time hearing how bad he is. How bad she is." Lucy shook her head and went on. "I can't think of my baby as an 'it' anymore, not after we've said all this stuff. But do you care? Does it matter what it turns out to be?"

Jake poured sand from one hand to the other. "Nooo," he said, speaking slowly. "Not really. It's just that maybe a girl—like her mother."

Lucy got up and brushed the sand off her clothes. She went to sit on the jetty, looking out at the ocean, before she turned back to face him. "I never thought of it like that before. Me being somebody's mother."

"Or me being somebody's father."

"Will we ever tell her? The baby, I mean," said Lucy.

"Tell her what?"

"About how you're not her real father."

"I'm going to be a *real* father, in the ways that matter. The same as you're going to be a *real* mother. Anyway, this baby has to know I *chose* her. Just as you and I chose each other."

"But you didn't choose me. Not really," said Lucy. "It was more like I just washed up on the shore and was there for you."

"Don't you ever say that," said Jake, taking his fist and slamming it into the palm of his other hand so that the noise it made was loud and sharp. "Don't you ever say that about yourself—that you washed up like a piece of seaweed. I chose you, Lucy Peale. And you chose me. And if we hadn't met that night up on the boardwalk in front of that stupid game with the cats and the garbage cans, then it'd've been somewhere else. I'm sure of it. If it hadn't been there, it'd've been in line for the Wild Mouse or at the Italian ice stand or looking at ourselves in those funky mirrors."

Lucy looked at him without blinking. Then she spun away, her shoes scratching against the sand. "Those mirrors made me look fat when I was thin. How d'you think I'd look in them now?"

"Beautiful—both of you," said Jake, reaching for her, placing one hand on her stomach, pulling her close with the other. "Oh, Lucy. Am I doing what I didn't want to do? Am I pressuring you?"

"Am *I* pressuring *you?*" said Lucy.

"Whatever it is—whatever's going on—I think it's the way it's meant to be," said Jake. "And afterwards—after the baby's here—when you've had time—when we're married—"

And for a minute neither of them could say anything, as

if what had happened between them was too important even to talk about.

"Come on, let's keep going," said Jake, turning the collar of her coat up against wind that had suddenly turned cold. "Here's the boardwalk already—another mile and we'll be home. Can you make it?"

"Yeah, sure," said Lucy, heading for the steps. "It's just that I'll probably sleep for a week after I get there."

"Well, before you settle in for your nap, let's talk about Thanksgiving."

"Thanksgiving?"

"Thanksgiving. You know, turkey. Anyway, my mother called this morning to see if I was coming home for the holiday and I told her I'd call her back, that I had this friend and— What do you think?"

"About what?"

"About going home for Thanksgiving."

"So go, then," said Lucy, hating the dull flat edge to her voice. "Why do I care what you do about Thanksgiving?"

"Not me, silly—us. I told you I told her I had a friend."

"Me?"

"You. So how about it, will you come?"

"Home with you for Thanksgiving?" she said, trying to keep from smiling. "To meet Emma and George and Meg and Tom and their kids?"

"And the dog," said Jake. "Don't forget the dog."

"Oh, yes, the dog. But I can't," said Lucy, her voice peaking, then fading away.

"Can't why?"

"Because look at me."

"Yeah?"

"I'm pregnant."

"I know that," said Jake.

"But they don't—and then they'll see—and they'll think—I just can't, is all."

"They have to know, Lucy. They're my family, and we're going to be a family, and it's all bound up together. Anyway, if I'm going to be a father, that makes them going to be grandparents and . . ."

"Not *really*," said Lucy.

"Really," said Jake.

"But they'll think I'm wild, that I'm—"

"They'll love you. Besides, they're not into making judgments, my folks aren't. Come on, here's a phone. We won't even wait till we get home." They crowded into a booth and Jake gave the operator his parents' number and asked her to charge the call to him at the apartment. Outside, on the edge of the boardwalk, two sea gulls tugged clumsily at an orange peel, waddling in circles, stopping from time to time to peck at the air. Inside, Jake and Lucy watched, rooting for first one and then the other as they waited for the call to go through. Then, all of a sudden, they began to laugh, rocking back and forth, holding each other up.

"Shhhh, it's ringing," said Jake, putting his hand over the mouthpiece and holding the receiver out for her to hear. Just then the ringing stopped and they heard the answering machine kick in on the other end. They listened to the recording of his mother's voice and waited for the beep before Jake said, "Hey, Mom, I'm just calling back to tell you 'yes' about Thanksgiving. Lucy and I'll be there.

Oh, and Mom, that's a name you'll all be hearing a lot of. Lucy . . . Lucy . . . Lucy . . . See you."

And then the laughter that they had been holding on to burst free and filled the booth and was swallowed up by the phone and carried out over the wire.

Ten

The laundromat opened at seven and Lucy was there, waiting, when the manager came to unlock the door.

"You're an early bird this morning," the woman said as she switched on the lights and turned up the heat. "I think of you as one of my afternoon people, coming like you usually do late in the day. I do that, some. Stuff people into pigeonholes. The early risers, the afternooners, the skin-of-the-teethers. They're the ones who come flying in here at the last minute and I'm near about *willing* these machines to go faster, so's I can close up and go home. Takes all kinds, though, I always say. Takes all kinds." She rubbed at the fronts of the dryers with a rag and came to stand beside Lucy, watching as she emptied her laundry basket into two side-by-side washers.

"So, what is it? You have the day off? Want to get an early start stuffing the turkey?"

"Turkey?" said Lucy, pushing her quarters into the slots and starting the machines. "I couldn't cook me any turkey. We do spaghetti, though, Jake and me. And grilled cheese and tuna casserole. And once even a chicken, except there was blood down in the far inside places near the bone and it like to made me throw up. Besides, we're going away for Thanksgiving. I have off from now till Monday, and so does Jake, and we're going down to Virginia today, to Smithfield, to his family's." She pulled her jacket around her and shivered—partly, she knew, because of the cold. And partly because of the trip.

"Sounds good," said the manager, heading for the door. "I'm off now, to get some breakfast, so in case I don't see you—eat a drumstick for me, kiddo."

When the woman had gone, Lucy went over to the bench and sat with her legs stretched out in front, her head back against the wall. As she listened to the rhythmic *swish-swish-swish* of the washing machines, her eyes closed and she felt herself starting to doze. Then suddenly she was wide awake. "Same as I was last night," she said out loud. "And the night before that, and the night before *that*. Every time I'd think about Virginia, and Jake's family, and me going to stay in their house. About Meg and Tom, and even the dog."

She took a deep breath, pushing air down into her lungs and trying to stop her heart from racing. "I can't go," she said. "And I can't not go. On account of them being Jake's family and him wanting to be with them, even though he did say we could stay here and eat Chinese carryout, if I really wanted. But I can't do that, either." She got up and started around the inside of the laundromat, walking faster and faster, running her fingers along cinder-block walls, the fronts of the machines. After a while she broke away and went to stand by the washers, leaning against them and feeling the vibration as the clothes spun crazily inside.

The machines stopped and the room was suddenly quiet. "Glory be," said Lucy into the silence. "In near about four hours we'll be leaving here for there. For Jake's house in Virginia. 'On the road by lunchtime' is what he said and . . ." She shook her head and reached in first one washer and then the other, dumping clothes into the basket and carrying it over to the dryer. She stood for a minute watching sheets and towels, underwear and jeans tumble around and around. She closed her eyes and saw again the pictures of Jake's family she had spread out on the kitchen table the night before.

"See, my mom's got crow's-feet, only she calls them laugh lines," Jake had said, coming to stand beside her. "How can you be afraid of someone with laugh lines? And my dad's getting bald on the top, kind of like a monk. Like St. Francis, maybe."

"Yes," Lucy had said, leaning close to study a picture of his mother and father at Meg's wedding, "but it's—you know." She put her hand on her stomach. "Me being pregnant and all. Do you think they'll notice?"

Jake had stood back, looking at her slowly and trying not to laugh. "They'll notice," he said, tugging at his face to keep from smiling. "They'll definitely notice."

"Maybe you should tell them. Give them some warning. You could call, say something. Say anything."

"I could," said Jake. "And maybe we should've except it's pretty late now and tomorrow's Wednesday and I know what my mom's like the day before a holiday. Back and forth between the shop and home, picking stuff up at the store, running around. And somehow this isn't a message for the answering machine. We'll play it by ear."

"It's not my ear I'm worried about," said Lucy, sliding the photographs into a pile.

Jake had come to stand behind her, rubbing her shoulders slowly, easing the tightness. "Look, Lucy, my folks are okay. They're pretty cool, actually. And if they're not all the way cool, they like to pretend they are, so they'll act that way, anyhow."

"You're sure?" said Lucy.

"Trust me," said Jake.

"Trust me," Lucy said now as she turned away from the dryer and went back to the bench. "Trust me, trust me, trust me." She reached in her pocket and pulled out a letter that had come for Jake from his mother just the other day. "Tell Lucy 'hello,'" the large, loopy writing said. "And that we can't wait to meet her."

"And I sort of maybe can't wait to meet them," said Lucy as she refolded the letter and put it in the envelope.

Jake was on the porch when Lucy got back from the laundromat. "You didn't have to do that," he said, taking the basket from her and carrying it into the apartment. "There's a washer and dryer at my parents' house. You could've taken your stuff and done it there. That's what

I'm going to do." He nodded at two duffel bags stuffed tight like sausages, sitting by the door.

"Yeah, right, Jake Jarrett. I'm going to arrive with my borrowed suitcase filled with dirty clothes. Anyway, I couldn't sleep."

"Again?"

"It's on account of those thoughts that all the time kept dancing in my head. About your folks, and the house, and those hundred million relatives."

"Well, you're in luck. This year the hundred million relatives are going to Aunt Margaret's house in Suffolk for Thanksgiving. You read Mom's letter. Though we'll probably stop in and see my grandparents over the weekend."

"Your grandparents?"

"Yeah, but not to worry," said Jake. "They're cool, too."

"And I know the rest—'trust me,' " said Lucy as she took her clean clothes from the basket and piled them into the suitcase.

"You got it," said Jake, taking a sweater out of her hand and putting it aside. "Come on, you can finish this later, but now let's go up to the beach. I always do that—whenever I'm heading away from here. Just stand and look at the ocean, and breathe it in."

Jake and Lucy stood on the jetty watching the waves. They stood with their arms around each other, feeling the unexpected warmth of the November sun, tasting a trace of salt on their lips.

"You know I really love our life," said Jake.

"Me, too," said Lucy. "And I don't want for it to ever have to change."

"It will, though," said Jake after a while. "You know that."

"Why will it?" Lucy twisted around to look at him. "We're happy the way we are now. We know what we want."

"Still, it'll change. Things always do," said Jake, looking down at her. "They're supposed to. It's like the shoreline here. Things happen to it, storms and tides and the wind. But, underneath, it's still the shoreline. It'll be that way with us, too. Stuff'll happen but—"

"What kind of stuff?"

"Just stuff."

"What kind?"

"Well, the baby for one."

"We know about the baby. What else?" said Lucy.

"Oh, different jobs someday. A new place to live. More kids. Maybe going back to school—for both of us," said Jake.

"I told you I wasn't much for school. That I was glad to be quit of it."

"Yeah, but you might change your mind. Don't you ever think of it? Doing something else?"

For a minute Lucy didn't say anything. Then, suddenly, the words came tumbling out. "I do. I think about it a lot, how I want a job where I'm not all the time cleaning up after people—scrubbing the slime off their bathtubs and picking up their trash. How I want to read all the books in the library and talk on the radio and work a computer. How I want to be a fisherman and a ballerina and maybe a paperhanger. And, most of all, how I want to know enough to teach somebody something someday. But it's scary, though. Just thinking about it."

"Yeah, it *is* scary. But we can do anything, Lucy."

"We can do anything," said Lucy, calling out over the sound of the waves.

"And right now what I want to do is get some doughnuts."

"Doughnuts?"

"I'm craving doughnuts," said Jake.

"I'm the one who's pregnant and *you're* craving doughnuts?"

"That's right. I didn't have any breakfast, did you?"

"I was too scared," said Lucy.

"Well, I have just the cure," said Jake. "Do you want chocolate or powdered sugar? Jelly-filled or custard? Come on." He grabbed her hand and together they jogged across the beach and over the boardwalk, down the side street to the doughnut shop on the highway.

"I'm never eating again," said Lucy as she licked the powdered sugar off her fingers and smoothed the front of her overalls, trying to decide if the two doughnuts she had just eaten made her look any more pregnant than she had before.

"Don't let my mother hear you say that," said Jake. "Especially when she trots out the turkey and cranberries and pumpkin pies with Cool Whip tomorrow, not to mention the sauerkraut and the sweet potatoes with marshmallows on top that nobody ever eats but her."

Lucy leaned back in the booth and rested her arms on

the bulge of her stomach. "You know what might be the best thing about being pregnant?" she said. "It's having someplace to rest your arms. A sort of a shelf. Anyway, I'm partial to sweet potatoes with marshmallows on top."

"She'll love you, then. My mom will. I mean, she would anyway, but having someone to help her eat up the sweet potatoes'll really cinch it. Come on, now, let's go."

For a minute Lucy caught hold of the table's edge. "Already?" she said. "It's way early yet."

"Well, yeah, but by the time we get home and get our stuff and load the car—and we have to stop for gas." He held out his hand to her, but Lucy shook her head at him, looking over her shoulder at the doughnuts piled on the counter.

"Maybe just one more," she said. "Or a cup of coffee. That's it. You need another cup of coffee for the ride. To keep you awake."

"I *am* awake," said Jake, opening his eyes as far as they would go and leaning close to her. "Remember, I *slept* last night. I didn't lie awake tossing and turning and then get up at dawn to do the wash."

"That's on account of you don't have to go off today and meet some strange family."

"My family's not strange."

"The family of some stranger, then."

"And I'm not a stranger."

"You know what I mean, Jake Jarrett."

"I know what you mean, Lucy Peale," said Jake, waiting as she slid out of the booth, then wrapping his arms around her and holding her close for a minute.

But once they were out of Ocean City and heading down Route 13 the feeling of panic swept over Lucy again. She looked at the stubbly fields stretching on either side of the highway and tried to imagine herself leaping out of the car and running across one of them, disappearing into the distance.

" 'Cept Jake'd come after me," she told herself.

They passed a bus stopped in front of a country store and she thought of asking Jake to let her off so she could go back the way she had come.

"But he never would," she whispered under her breath. "He'd turn the car around instead and take me back to the apartment, the two of us together." She closed her eyes and saw Jake's mother's dining-room table heaped high with turkey and cranberries, with sauerkraut and sweet potatoes with marshmallows on top. "And us not there to eat it," she said.

"What?" said Jake, turning toward her.

"Oh, nothing," said Lucy. " 'Cept aren't we maybe going to be too early?"

"Early for what?"

"For getting there."

"It's home, for gosh sakes, Lucy, and you can't be too early for home."

They stopped at a gas station so that Lucy could go to the bathroom and when she came out she stood looking at the weathered buildings lining the road. "Maybe we could go somewhere, sightsee, or something, on account of I've never been this way before."

"In Belle Haven? Sightsee? There's nothing here besides the cemetery," said Jake.

"We could see that," said Lucy, getting in the car and fastening her seat belt.

"We could," said Jake, "just as long as *you* know that *I* know foot-dragging when I see it." He turned the car away from the highway, past houses with wrap-around porches and trees tall and stark against the winter sky to the cemetery at the far side of town.

"It's pretty," said Lucy, rolling down the car window, then opening the door and getting out, making her way along the rows of tombstones. "And quieter'n anything I've ever heard before."

They walked for a while without saying anything, reading the markers and watching as a turkey buzzard circled the sky. "It's nice, sort of," said Lucy. "The way the fields come right up to the edge of the graveyard here, without any fence, like what is and what isn't are all one together."

"The past and the present."

"It puts me in mind some of Hector and Presilla—all these people here. How they were and then weren't. Aren't anymore, except they are, somehow. Somewhere. I have to think on it like that, don't you?"

"Yes," said Jake, reaching for her hand and feeling her fingers cold against his. "Yes."

They stopped for lunch and again on the Bridge-Tunnel, pulling onto the parking lot and going to stand at the rail. "It's called Hampton Roads, this part," said Jake. "Where the ocean meets the Chesapeake Bay. And years ago, when my folks were little, there used to be ferries taking people back and forth, and my grandmother always got seasick and then had to eat nothing but baked potatoes for the whole day afterwards to settle her stomach. At least, that's the way she tells it now."

"What's she like? Your grandmother?"

"Little and wiry and always wearing high heels and earrings and with a collection of elephants on every surface of her house. And she reads a lot."

"Is she scary?"

"My grandmother? No way, not unless she draws her mouth into a thin, straight line. *That's* when you know to watch out. But usually not for long."

Lucy turned away from him, looking out to sea, but all around her the faces of stern-looking women with thin, straight mouths seemed to stare at her. "Does she have beady eyes?" she said.

"Who?"

"Your grandmother."

"No way, José. They're—just eyes, with wrinkles around them. Crow's-feet, like my mother's, only more so. Now come on, Lucia. This three-and-a-half-hour trip has already taken four and we're not there yet."

"Here's the water tower," said Jake, pointing through the early November dark to the silvery tower. "Every time when I was little and we went anywhere—even if it was just to the next town over—I always knew we were home when I spotted it."

"Are we?" said Lucy, her voice catching. "Home, I mean."

"Almost," said Jake. "Just time for a respectable countdown." And he cleared his throat and started, "Ten—nine—eight—"

"Slower," said Lucy.

"Se-ven—" said Jake, slowing the car to a crawl as he dragged out the words. "Siiix—fiiive—"

Lucy's palms began to sweat and she rolled down the window, letting the cool outside air wash over her.

"Fo-ur, thr-ee."

"Tw-o-o-o," whispered Lucy.

"One," Jake sang out as he swung the car off the road and down onto the driveway in front of a large brick house that seemed aglow with lights. And suddenly there were people spilling out the front door, down off the porch, and swarming around the car.

"It's Jake—and Lucy," they all seemed to call at once. A black dog barked and jumped up against the side of the car, poking his head through the open window and looking at Lucy.

"Oh, Lord, they're all here," said Jake. "Even Homewood. Mom, Dad, Meg, and the kids." He gestured to the three little girls dancing in the headlights. "Everybody but Tom."

"And the hundred million relatives," said Lucy.

"And the hundred million relatives," said Jake, leaning across her and pushing at the dog. "Down, Homewood. Give Lucy a break."

She watched as he opened the door on his side, calling back to her, "Hang loose, I'll come get you." She heard the voices swirling around: "Have a good trip? Much traffic? We're *so* glad to see you . . ." She watched as he scooped

134

up the oldest child and put her on his shoulders, as he came around the car.

Lucy opened her door and got out, rubbing the small of her back.

Jake held out his hand to her but just then the child on his shoulders lunged forward, pointing and calling out, "Hey, Nana, everybody, here's Lucy and she's got a baby in her stomach."

Eleven

"She does, doesn't she?" the child asked, her voice breaking into the silence that hung suddenly over the driveway. "I know it because she's fat and when Mommy was fat like that it was because she had Minnie in *her* stomach and before that Annie and before that me, Elizabeth, only I don't remember that part."

"You remember enough, Elizabeth," said Jake, laughing as he swung the child off his shoulders. "And you're right. Lucy does have a baby in her stomach."

"What can I say?" said a young woman, stepping forward and shaking her head. "I'm Meg and these are my children, only sometimes, like right this minute, I don't always claim them. I'm glad to meet you, though, and now we're going home, but we'll be back for dinner tomorrow—preferably with tape across their mouths. Anyway, congratulations, you guys, but you could've said something, Bro."

No, Lucy wanted to cry. It's not to do with Jake. But before she could say anything she saw his mother and father coming toward her, holding out their hands. "Lucy, we're so glad to meet you," said Emma Jarrett. "So glad to have you here, aren't we, George?"

"Yes, yes, indeed." Jake's father spoke quickly, then stopped, and for a minute Lucy could see the two of them looking everywhere but at her stomach, could hear their unasked questions. Then they all spoke at once.

"Was there traffic?" asked Emma.

"How's the car holding up?" asked George.

"I guess we should've said something," said Jake, his voice riding over the others. "Should've called back—"

"Except as how Jake said it wasn't any message for an answering machine, or maybe the phone either one," said Lucy.

"Well, good news is always better in person," said Emma, putting her arm around Lucy and steering her up on the porch. "And a new grandchild is definitely good news."

They moved into the hall, Jake and his father dropping the luggage at the foot of the stairs. "Now, Jake, if you'd just take that stuff upstairs—I've put Lucy in Meg's old room, but maybe now, maybe we should, I mean, maybe because of the—" She stopped and ran her fingers through her hair. "Oh, I don't know—it's just that—"

"Don't sweat it, Mom," said Jake, slinging his duffel bags over his shoulder and picking up Lucy's suitcase. "I'll figure it out."

"No," said Lucy, reaching for her suitcase and holding it up in front of her. "No. I mean not yet, till first I get to say what I've got to say on account of Jake won't, 'cause he's too nice, and it's just hanging there, waiting to be said. About how this baby's got nothing to do with Jake. Nothing to do with you. This baby's got to do with somebody whose name I won't say out loud ever again. This baby's got to do with what happened before I even *knew* Jake, when I was still over to the Church of the Saving Grace and Pa found out and said as how I'd have to stand up there for all to see and say how I was bad clear through and I never would. I never could."

She held tighter to the suitcase as she went on. "And then I went into town and that's when I met Jake up on the boardwalk and he followed me down on the beach and got me food and said if I ever needed a place to stay and I did. On account of the storm. And after that it got for me and Jake like it was meant to be, like we'd known each other forever and always would, and like the baby was a part of *us*. And it got so we wanted this baby more'n anything and figure on getting married and someday we'll have us a house and a rake and an attic. It got so we wanted to have it and raise it and buy it school shoes and a backpack so's it could see the falling stars and the sun come up, and take it to the Grand Canyon maybe someday. And we wanted it to know a God who was slow to anger and filled with love, same as we were, only about a million times more. On account of that's the way it is with God."

Lucy stopped and there was no sound in the hall but the ticking of the grandfather clock. She slid the suitcase down over her stomach and dropped it on the floor. "Oh, glory, Jake, did I say it all wrong?" she asked.

"You said it just right," he said, reaching out to touch her on the point of her chin.

"And, far as I can see, that makes us honorary grandparents, to say the least," said George, picking up the suitcase and moving it out of the way.

"Yes," said Emma. "Especially since you two are talking about a house and a rake and an attic someday."

"And now," said Jake. "What's for supper?"

When Lucy woke the next morning the room was dark and shadowed. She lifted her head and listened to the sound of rain against the windowpanes, then burrowed deeper in bed, trying to drift back into sleep. But she was wide awake and in a few minutes she was up, easing open the door to the hall and sniffing at the smell of coffee. Pulling on her robe and a pair of socks, she made her way down the stairs, walking quietly and not sure whether she was too early or too late. "Too early or too late for what?" she asked herself and when she got to the bottom she turned toward the room at the back of the house where they had been the night before.

"Good morning," said Emma, looking up from the crossword puzzle she was doing. "Did you sleep well?"

"*Oh, yes,*" said Lucy, surprising herself with the way her voice seemed to carry through the silent house. "I mean, better'n I have for ages, better'n I have since before Jake and I decided we'd come here for Thanksgiving and not stay home and eat Chinese carryout, on account of once we *did* say we'd come, then I started in to not being able to sleep and imagining what it'd be like and thinking about you and Mr. Jarrett and Meg and Tom and the kids and even the dog and the hundred million relatives—" She stopped short, feeling for a minute that she had reached the top of a high ladder and didn't know how to get down.

"Yes." Emma laughed, taking off her glasses and rubbing her eyes. "*Other* people's families are always scary, except that the person who belongs to them never thinks so—if you see what I mean. The first time I went to dinner at George's parents', I was scared to death—and I'd known them all my life. George never did understand that."

"Like Jake," said Lucy. "He allowed as how you all weren't scary. How you had crow's-feet and a bald spot—Mr. Jarrett, I mean. How you were cool."

"We work at it," said Emma.

"He said that, too. How you and Mr. Jarrett try to be cool and so even if you weren't all the way you'd act like you were, so it'd be the same thing anyway."

"He knows us pretty well, Jake does," said Emma, laughing again and wiping tears out of the corners of her eyes. "Now, how about some breakfast?"

But Lucy had moved forward into the room and was standing at the back wall that, the night before, had been covered with curtains. "It's windows," she said, "and there's water down there. Is it a river?"

"No," said Emma, coming to stand beside her. "It's Cypress Creek, but when the kids were little, it could just as well have been the Amazon, or the Congo, or the Mississippi, the way they were always setting off to explore something. Especially Jake."

"I wish I'd known him then," said Lucy. "That's the thing about somebody—loving them, I mean. It's sort of like going in in the middle of a movie when you can't ever go back to the start and catch up. I want to know *all* of Jake."

"Watch out what you wish for," said Emma, getting up and leading the way into the kitchen. "It's all there on film, on slides, actually. From when Meg was a baby up through Minnie's second birthday just last month. And George'd love to show it to you."

"Would he?" said Lucy. "Do you think?"

"I know he would. Maybe tonight, after dinner. He even thought about getting a video camera, until we rented one last Christmas and found that it told us more than we really wanted to know. More than we really wanted to save, I guess. That's why we like the slides, and George is so good at capturing just the moment of things. Now, what would you like for breakfast?"

While Emma put cereal and juice and bagels out on the counter, Lucy went to stand at the dining-room door, looking down at the table already set, and counting to herself. "That's a lot of people," she said, turning back into the kitchen.

"Just the four of us, and Meg and Tom and the kids. Oh, yes, I almost forgot. Jake's grandparents are coming, too. As soon as they heard Jake was bringing you for the weekend, they begged off of going to my sister-in-law's and decided to come here instead. My mother-in-law's an incurable romantic."

"Oh," said Lucy, sitting down heavily on a kitchen chair. "The grandmother with the elephants on the tabletops and the mouth that sometimes gets into a thin, straight line and when it does you have to watch out—but just for a while?"

"That's the one," said Emma. "In fact, she's the only one; my parents are both dead."

"Oh," said Lucy again. "I mean, I'm sorry, but what about—you know—" She rested her arms on her stomach and rocked back and forth.

"The baby?" said Emma. "I already told her. I called last night, just to give her a chance to get used to the idea."

"What'd she say?"

"Nothing, at first."

"Was that on account of she was drawing her mouth into a thin, straight line?" said Lucy.

"Probably," said Emma. "But *then* she said—and here I could just see her pulling herself up to her full five feet two inches—'Well, these things happen and more power to them.' So don't worry, Lucy. Though I know that's easy for *me* to say."

"Well, I won't. I'll try not, leastways. But the thing is, Jake's grandmother shouldn't worry either, on account of it not being Jake's baby and us not sleeping together—Jake and me. I mean, we never did. Not even the once—not even the time I— That's because of Jake and him saying as how I had too much going on in my life and too much stuff to sort out. That's how come we're waiting till *after* the baby to get married. So's we'll be sure we're sure."

Just then the teakettle shrieked and Lucy looked up, her face flushing a bright pink. "I shouldn't've ought to said that, should I? About how Jake and I don't—you know.

Shouldn't've said what has to do with just the two of us together."

"Probably not," said Emma.

"And maybe if Jake knew—I mean, maybe it'd be better—"

"I didn't hear a thing, Lucy. What with the teakettle making all that racket, and the rain on the windowpanes," Emma said. "Come along, I'll get a tray and you can take your breakfast to the porch. I declare, I don't know what we did before we added that room. We practically *live* there now."

Dinner was over. The slide show was over. Everyone had gone home and George and Emma, after sitting and talking for a few minutes, had gone up to bed. Jake and Lucy sat on the couch together, watching a movie on video.

"I can't believe you never saw *Annie Hall*," said Jake. "Are you getting into it? The way you almost have to lean forward to catch what they're saying, because except when Alvie's talking right to us we get more from eavesdropping than anything else. The way they just *are* because they *are* rather than existing as part of a movie with a mind to the audience. It's what I think Woody Allen does best—sort of dumps it there and shrugs as if to say, 'Here it is, take what you want.' What d'you think?"

"I like the girl."

"Annie?"

"Yeah," said Lucy. "I like her clothes and her hats and the way if it was summer and she was at Ocean City she'd never be all tan with long blond hair. I liked the part about

143

the lobsters and the books—except when I moved in with you I didn't *have* any books, but if I had I'd've brought them and we could've put them side by side or maybe, on account of the way you are about your books, on separate shelves together. But now I think we should rewind and start again."

"Again?" said Jake. "Don't you want to get to the end before we start again? To see how it comes out?"

"Yeah, well, except I wasn't one hundred percent paying attention and this time I would. I mean, I'd lean forward like you said and just *be* there."

"Hey, Lucia, this could be important to our whole relationship. Hang on a minute—I need refueling." He got up and went to the kitchen and Lucy heard the refrigerator door open, heard him call, "You want anything?"

"No, thanks," answered Lucy, still feeling comfortable and full and almost sleepy. In a minute Jake was back with a glass of milk and a plate of bread dressing.

"You sure?" he said. "About the bread dressing, I mean. It's even better cold. Now, let's get back to this. Here *I* am a professed Woody Allen fan, and here *you* are with your first run-through of *Annie Hall*, and you tell me you weren't one hundred percent paying attention. This could be serious, you know."

Lucy blinked and leaned forward, saw Jake put his hand up to his mouth and turn away. "You're funnin' me, Jake Jarrett."

"Yeah, maybe a little. But, anyway, how come you weren't into it?"

"Because I was thinking."

"About what?"

"Well, not so much thinking as telling," said Lucy.

"Telling what?" said Jake.

"Everything. The way it happened. The whole day. Don't you do that some? Like if you've been somewhere special and you want to keep remembering it, but it's more than just thinking on it. It's *telling*."

"To someone?" said Jake. "Do you tell it *to* someone?"

"To Doris. My sister. I always pretend I'm telling it all to her and doing so makes it seem to sit firmer in my head, and besides, for a while then at least, I can pretend that things're the same as they were before. Between the two of us. Doris and me."

"Show me," said Jake, reaching for her hand and locking her fingers in his. "Or tell me, the way you would if you were describing being here."

"Well," said Lucy, "it'd just be the today part, because I told the yesterday part last night. I do it mostly then, when I'm just getting on to sleep."

"Okay, the today part, then. What would you say?"

"First I'd tell about getting up early this morning and how it was just me and your mother downstairs and—"

"No, say it like you would, not as if you're telling me about telling it. As if it's just you, inside your head."

"You won't laugh?"

"I won't laugh," said Jake.

Lucy took a deep breath and let it out all at once. "Well," she said, taking another breath and feeling for a minute the way she used to feel in grade school when she had to stand up in front of the class and recite. "The table was set like in a magazine, with candles and flowers and napkins so big you could've made a bathing suit out of one of them and still had goods left over to spare. And mostly during the day we just hung out and watched the rain and smelled the turkey cooking. But then when it stopped some—the rain, not the turkey—we went outside and squished our way down the steps to the creek and Jake told me about when he was little and about the raft he and these guys tried to build and how he liked to think he was Tom Sawyer or Huckleberry Finn. And the way he made it sound, I went right upstairs and added them to the list of books I want to read.

"When it was nearly time for dinner, Meg and Tom and the children and Jake's grandparents came all at the same time, and for a while the grownups sat in the living room, while the kids mostly ran around in circles. Jake's grandfather is tall with silvery-gray hair and he shook my hand and said he hoped he'd be seeing lots more of me. His grandmother is small, like a bird, with earrings and high heels, the way Jake said she'd be. She took me over to the love seat by the window and sat beside me and said how I was a healthy-looking girl and sure to have a healthy baby and that was what mattered most and was I any kin to the Peales over Suffolk way. I said 'no' and held my breath, hoping she wouldn't ask me any more questions, and she didn't, 'cause right then she started in to talk about Jake when he was little and about her garden and told me how when Jake and I got a garden we should be sure and come and dig up some of her daylilies.

"At dinner I sat between Jake and his father and before we ate we all held hands and said grace. Then we had a feast with turkey and bread dressing and cranberry sauce. With peas and sauerkraut and rolls and sweet potatoes with marshmallows on the top. With salad and olives and pickles and pumpkin pie. Everybody had some of everything, except for the sweet potatoes—and Emma and I had them mostly to ourselves. Once we were done we sat at the table for a long time and talked, but not the kids, on account of they were off in the other room watching *Madeline* on video.

"Afterwards we helped with the dishes and Homewood ate turkey scraps out of his bowl and everybody was there sort of bumping into each other and it was nice and not at all scary, the way I thought it'd be. Not even the grandmother part."

Lucy stopped for a minute to catch her breath, but when Jake started to say something, she held up her hand. "No, wait, I'm not done yet—and this is the place where you have to promise not to laugh—because when I'm telling it to Doris in my head I always finish up by saying how I wish she could meet you someday and see what it's like for us and what it's like to love someone—and to have him love you back."

"Oh, Lucy," said Jake, pulling her close.

"So, Lucy, what've you guys done all weekend?" asked Meg as they waited in her kitchen for Jake and Tom to come back with pizza.

"Well," said Lucy, lifting the lid off the box of baby clothes that Meg had dragged down from the attic, and slipping a yellow bootie over her fingers, "today we went over to Williamsburg and walked around a spell. And yesterday Jake showed me your mother's shop and this really old church and the hardware store where he used to work

147

in the summertime and then we drove out to where he went to high school. But mostly we watched movies— *Annie Hall* and *Hannah and Her Sisters* and *Manhattan*."

"Oh, Lord," said Meg. "Jake's on his Woody Allen kick again. Did it ever occur to you, Lucy, that this brother of mine has some real obsessions—Woody Allen, writing, the ocean, and the books of Adrian Blair. And speaking of Adrian Blair—whatever happened about the dogsbody job?"

"Dogsbody," said Lucy. She repeated the word slowly. "Dogsbody."

"Yes, you know how he got the job lined up with Adrian Blair for when the great man's on his writer-in-residence stint at Hopkins. And how the job description is 'basic drudge.' He told you, didn't he? I mean, I'd never have mentioned it—I mean, maybe he's changed his mind— isn't going to—now that you all are—"

Lucy sat for a while without saying anything, and when she spoke, her voice was small and rushed. "He told me, but it was the second day from when I met him and ages back, before the time I ever dreamed that Jake'd matter to me, or me to him. I'd been sleeping most of the day, in his apartment, and when he came home we started in to talk about stuff: about school and how he'd dropped out but maybe one day he'd go back. About how he really liked the books of this famous English writer and how when he found out he was coming Jake asked if he could come back and take his classes and the people at Hopkins said no on account of he never graduated and these were something called graduate courses. And how after that Jake just wrote a letter to Adrian Blair all the way in England and told him about it and Mr. Blair wrote back and said on account of him being handicapped, sort of, and needing help with things, would he be interested in the job of dogsbody, which Jake said was what you said—a drudge. And in between how maybe they could talk writing some, and books, too."

She looked up, her eyes wide and dark. "And how it'd be sure to be the greatest thing in his whole life and better'n a whole bunch of college degrees. Especially with him wanting to be a writer and all.

"And I forgot," said Lucy, her voice cracking and tears filling her eyes. "Because he never mentioned it again and there was stuff going on and I never thought—" She shook her head and turned away, staring hard at the crayon pictures stuck all over Meg's refrigerator.

"And it's soon, isn't it?" said Lucy, swallowing hard and trying to keep her voice steady.

"Yes," said Meg. "Just after the first of the year, I think. But maybe he's—"

Just then they heard a car door slam and the sound of Jake and Tom coming across the driveway. Lucy reached out and caught Meg by the wrist. "Don't say anything, please," she whispered. "I have to think on this some."

Twelve

Lucy carried her suitcase down the steps and dropped it by the kitchen door next to Jake's duffel bags and Emma's care package filled with ham and turkey sandwiches, grapes, and a whole frozen spinach lasagna.

"Well, Lucy," said Emma, "it's been grand having you here. Grand getting to know you."

"Oh, yes," said Lucy. "I mean, for *me*, to *be* here. Like it was something out of a book, or a magazine. It's been—" She held up her hands as if catching at words. "Like you said—grand. For me, anyway."

"Couldn't you all stay—just till tomorrow?" said Emma. "There'll be so much traffic this afternoon, what with it being Sunday of the Thanksgiving weekend."

"Thanks, Mom, but we've got to be heading back. Besides, Lucy has to be at work early tomorrow," said Jake.

"I was lucky they even let me off this weekend, on account of the hotel being near about full and all. But Jessie Penny wanted extra work and Mrs. Ayres, the housekeeper, said she could do my shifts. But just through today."

"So we'd better get started," said Jake. "Because, with that crib, we'll have to take it a little slower."

Lucy looked out at the crib Jake and his father had lashed on the top of the Toyota and thought how just seeing it there suddenly made the baby seem realer than it had before.

"I put the other stuff inside," Jake went on. "The car seat, the Kanga-Rocka-Roo, the box of clothes. See—I told you Meg's basement was a gold mine, and there's more where that came from—the playpen, the high chair, and even something that hangs from the doorframe and jounces."

"Yes," said Lucy, her eyes wide. "It was like the time I went into the Sears store over in Salisbury and wandered through the baby department, running my hands along the cribs, poking at the mobiles and making them spin, and trying to imagine *real* babies and one of them belonging to us. It was that way last night over at Meg and Tom's, only this time there they both were, saying 'Take this, and this, and boy, we'd never have made it without *this*.' "

"And they're glad for you to have it, peace knows," said Emma. "It's a shame you don't have room to take the swing, but you can get it next time you come."

"Or we might even bring it to you," said George. "Emma's always up for a weekend at the Beach Place. Right?"

"Hmmm, yes," said Emma. "I love hotels."

151

"Does it make you sad?" asked Lucy, twisting in her seat and watching as the town disappeared behind them.

"What, leaving?" said Jake.

"Yes," said Lucy. "I mean, I never was anywhere that I cared about not being anymore. Until now. And it feels sort of—makes me feel almost—"

"Sore inside," said Jake.

"Yes," said Lucy, swallowing carefully. "Like with something that hurts and you keep pushing at it to see if it still hurts and to see if it's gone away, both at the same time."

"I feel that way every time I leave my parents' house," said Jake. "And it's not that I want to *be* there permanently, not that I want to *live* there. And by the time I get to the Bridge-Tunnel I'm over it and thinking about all the stuff I have to do at home. But for a while it's sad."

"For them, too, do you think? Your folks, I mean."

"Yeah," said Jake. "I think, 'cause once I forgot something and had to go back and there was Dad hacking at a flower bed that didn't have a weed in sight, and Mom was sitting on the back steps holding a mug of coffee, with tears running down her face. And the thing was, she didn't act embarrassed or say 'Aren't I silly' or anything, but she didn't wipe them away, either. Then we talked for another few minutes, and when I finally left, it was sad all over again. But tell me—what'd you think? Of the family, I mean."

"Oh," said Lucy. "I liked them. I liked them all. I liked your mother and father and Meg and Tom and the kids. I liked your grandmother and the way she said she'd teach me to grow a plant from an avocado seed and that we should take some of her daylilies if we ever have a house, and some of her lilies of the valley, too, and the way, when we went to visit, your grandfather played his record of a thunderstorm for me and said as how you used to like it when you were a little kid and how it was the best way ever to have a thunderstorm. On a record, I mean. And I liked the way your grandparents liked me, even though I could tell right off that they wished that things were different between us and how maybe it would be better if there wasn't any baby quite yet, and if there was, that it was yours and not—somebody else's."

"How many times do I have to tell you? It'll *be* mine, Lucia."

"And I liked your house and the creek and watching your father's slides and how after that it was almost like knowing you clear through. I liked *Annie Hall* and Homewood and seeing where you went to school and your mother's shop and all the stuff she had in it. And I liked going to church and the way it made me feel that it was okay for me to be there. And that God thought so, too."

Lucy stopped and put her head back on the seat, staring up at the dome light overhead.

I said I'd think on it, but I can't, she thought. On account of it's being too big—this thing about Jake having a chance at some best-in-the-whole-world job and him having to go, and take it, and me knowing that, except every time I think on it some, I go all cold and squishy inside. She closed her eyes and felt the tears press against her lids. She opened her mouth and breathed deeply. The baby kicked and she rested her hand on her stomach, trying to imagine an elbow, a knee, a tiny heel.

"You okay?" said Jake as he spun the radio dial until he picked up a football game.

"Hmmmm," said Lucy. She turned her head to the side, away from Jake, and watched the scenery rush by in a blur of tears. The announcer's voice filled the car and seemed both close at hand and far away.

They went across the Bridge-Tunnel and headed up through the Eastern Shore of Virginia and into Maryland, stopping once at a restaurant so that Lucy could run in to the bathroom, while Jake huddled over the radio waiting for the Redskins to make a touchdown.

"I can't," Lucy said to herself when they were back on the road, not daring to think what it was she couldn't do. I can't, I can't, I can't, she thought again, the words humming in her head like tires on the highway. I can't, I can't, I can't.

Jake slowed the car at a roadside stand, but when he looked over at Lucy, she turned the other way and he speeded up again. She closed her eyes, blotting out the flat brown countryside, but soon thoughts of Jake and the job and of herself overwhelmed her and she opened them again just as they trundled over the bridge into Ocean City.

"We're home," shouted Jake.

"Yes," said Lucy, but when she spoke her voice sounded small and unused.

"Got to see the ocean," he said, pulling the car onto a side street and parking close to the boardwalk. "See if it's still there. Come on."

But Lucy hung back, standing on the street and leaning on the boardwalk, watching as Jake ran down to the water's edge, hearing him call out, "Hey, we're back. Lucy and I're back."

"Is anything wrong?" asked Jake when they had finished the turkey and ham sandwiches that Emma had sent along. "You've hardly said a word since we left Smithfield, and what you *have* said would never make it in the dialogue department. I mean, if I used it in a story—" He pulled an exaggerated frown and shrugged at her.

"Well, I'm sorry, Mr. Jake Jarrett," said Lucy. "Sorry that what I have to say doesn't sound like something out of some book somewhere. Sorry it's just plain old everyday kind of conversation. I didn't know I had to talk special so's you could *use* it. I didn't know you were *listening*, 'cept in the way people listen to people when they listen. I didn't know—"

"Hey, Lucy, come on. Just kidding. Lighten up. I only wanted to know if anything was wrong, that's all."

"No." Lucy gathered up her dishes and took them over to the sink, turning on the water full-force and adding detergent, watching as the bubbles crowded one on top of another. "No," she said again.

"You sure?"

"Yes." She pushed her hands down into the water, wincing at the heat but refusing to add any cold.

"You're sure you're sure?"

"I'm sure," said Lucy. And then, without meaning to, she swung around, her hands dripping soapsuds down the front of her overalls and on the floor. "I'm sure. Except that I've been trying to think on it all day, and last night too, and I couldn't get a hold of it, like maybe it was a greased pig or something."

"Think about what? Get hold of what?" said Jake.

"The dogsbody job and how I *forgot*. I mean, here it is the most important thing in your whole entire life and glory-be-to-God special and I *forgot*. And I kept on forgetting till just last night when Meg said what she did. When she asked me about it and when it started, up there in Baltimore, and then I remembered. And it's im-por-tant."

"Not that important," said Jake, coming to stand in front of her and taking her soapy hands in his. "Besides, I'm not going. I've decided."

"You have to go," said Lucy, and then, because the words sounded frayed, she said them again. "You have to go."

"I don't have to go," said Jake. "I'll write a letter to Adrian Blair and explain everything, about you, and the baby, and our situation."

"No," said Lucy. "On account of he's *expecting* you, he *needs* you, and besides, I don't much like being a *situation*."

"*You're* not a situation, we *have* one," said Jake. "And besides, Mr. Blair can get someone else. Anybody'd jump at that job. There must be a dozen people, twenty maybe."

"See," said Lucy. "See. That's because it *is* glory-be-to-God special. Like I said."

"Well, you'll go with me, then," said Jake. "I'm supposed to have a room in the place the university's renting for him, and you'll just go with me."

"I can't," said Lucy. "On account of the baby. And the crib and the Kanga-Rocka-Roo. I just can't move in with this man who's important and famous and has a job to do, and me being nothing to him. I reckon I know what's right, and that's not. Right, I mean."

"We'll get our own place, then. Baltimore's full of apartments, especially down near Hopkins. We'll check with off-campus housing. And I'll just run back and forth."

"You're not to do with the university," said Lucy. "You're to do with Adrian Blair." She wanted to go on: to say that Mr. Blair was counting on him to drive him places, to help with the wheelchair; to say that Jake was there to learn about writing, in between times. But a sudden tiredness settled over her and Lucy slumped against the refrigerator, feeling the cool smoothness of the door on her face.

Jake took her by the arm and led her into the living room, easing her into a chair while he pulled out the sofa bed, got the pillows from the closet. "We'll talk about it tomorrow," he said as Lucy leaned back, looking at the wall over the bed, at Hector and Presilla and the fat white cat staring back at her.

The next morning Lucy was still tired. "Tired from thinking," she said to herself as she pushed her housekeeping cart along the hotel corridor. "And tired from not thinking."

She let herself into one of the unoccupied rooms on the ninth floor, sitting on the edge of the bed and stretching her legs out in front of her, staring at the darkened television screen, glad of the blankness of the empty room. "Not like back at the apartment where things sort of tangle me around," she said out loud. "Like Jake saying I should go to Baltimore with him, or how he maybe won't go at all. How it's not important, only I know it is."

Except even Presilla knows it won't work, she thought as she got up and smoothed the bed before going to stand at the sliding glass door, looking out at the lowering sky. And so does Hector, and the fat white cat. They all three know about how this job's important for Jake and how he'd come not to like me anymore and I'd come not to like myself. If I went with him or kept him from going, either one. And how it'd be something grown up between us and years from now we'd still be aiming to find a way around it.

"But I'm scared of being alone," she whispered into the empty room. "Scared in a way I wasn't ever before, even when I left home and the Church of the Saving Grace and came over here to Ocean City all by myself. But then I met Jake and now I can't think of not having him and him not having me and us not having each other."

"Except I have to," said Lucy as she went through the rest of the rooms, changing sheets, putting out fresh towels, running the vacuum cleaner.

"Except I have to," she said as she walked along the beach that afternoon, waiting for Jake to leave for work; as she went home and fixed her supper and sat pushing the pile of scrambled eggs around the plate.

"Except I have to," she said as she went over to the telephone, and sat twisting her hands.

When her father answered the phone, Lucy hung up, then sat for a minute, breathing quickly and watching the sweat that skimmed the palms of her hands. Then she called again, punching out the numbers and holding the receiver at arm's length as she stared down into it.

"Praise the Lord." Her father's voice rolled up and she jumped and moved as if to push the phone away, to leave it lying there on the table, abandoned.

"Praise the Lord," he said again.

"It's me, Pa." Lucy swallowed and started over, forcing her voice to sound larger, stronger. "It's me, Pa, Lucy Peale, and I called to talk to Doris."

What if he hangs up, Lucy thought. What if he's *already* hung up. She strained to block out the sounds in the apartment—the hum of the refrigerator, the drip of water in the kitchen sink—to see if they were still connected. Then she heard him put the receiver down, heard his footsteps, slow and heavy, on the floor.

"Is it you, Lucy?" said Doris. "Is it really you?"

"It's me," said Lucy.

"Don't say anything," said Doris. "Not until I move." And Lucy closed her eyes and imagined her sister pulling the telephone cord around the door of the kitchen and into the hall. "Now," said Doris, "what's wrong. Is it to do, you know, with the baby? Is it to do with that? I waited to hear from you, after you left. I wished for there to be a card, a letter. And once, even, I went into Ocean City with a girl from work and thought maybe I'd see you, on account of where else would you know to go, but when we got there everything was closed up tight and the sand sort of pushed around the broadwalk and she got spooked and we went along home. But tell me, what about the baby?"

"Nothing *to* tell," said Lucy, " 'cept I look like I swallowed a watermelon and Jake tells me he *likes* the way I

look and that pregnant women are beautiful and sometimes, after he's said that, I run and sneak a look in the
mirror and maybe he's right, just a little."

"Who's Jake?" said Doris.

"Jake's—Jake," said Lucy, "and he's different from anybody I ever met before, or you either, I reckon. And sometimes, at night before I go to sleep, I make like I'm telling
you about him: how he's wonderful and sort of funny and
how he writes stories that'll one day be books; how when
he was little he made a raft on account of he wanted to be
Huckleberry Finn."

"He's not, he wasn't the one, you know, last spring
who—"

"*No,*" said Lucy. "Except Jake's said about a million
times over how he's going to be the father to my baby—
the real father—real in every way but one. He goes with
me to the doctor, to the childbirth classes, and helps me
with my breathing, and we already have a crib and a
T-shirt that says *Beach Baby* for next summer. But it's the
in-between time I need to talk to you about."

"Yes," said Doris. "When?"

"Quick, soon, tomorrow maybe, before I lose my nerve
and hang on," said Lucy. "Besides, I can drive now, so's I
can pick you up when I get off from work and bring you
here and show you where we live and all."

"I have to," said Lucy when Jake got home from work
the next night. She was sitting at the kitchen table folding
a paper towel into squares and trying to think of how to
say what she had to say.

"Have to what?" said Jake.

"Have to have you go to Baltimore to work for Adrian Blair and have to have me stay home. Here, in Ocean City."

"No," said Jake. "I told you the other night, you'll come with me."

"And I told you no, I can't, but mostly then it was saying I can't the way a person says I can't right off, without thinking it all the way clear through. Only now I have."

"But, Lucy—"

Lucy shook her head and put her hand up. "You've got to let me say it straight out, Jake Jarrett. About how you told me once I have a lot of stuff to sort through and you're not going to pressure me. And how you have stuff to sort through, too, and promises to keep, both to Adrian Blair and to you yourself. And how we've got to hang on to each other by letting each other go, so it won't always and forever after be like some weed growing up between us."

"I'll work with Adrian Blair another time," said Jake.

"There won't *be* another time," said Lucy. "You said so yourself. You said how Mr. Blair's getting old and how his health's not so good and how this's the chance of a lifetime. That's what you said."

"That's a cliché," said Jake. "Did I *really* say that?"

"Yes," said Lucy.

"Well, chance of a lifetime or not, I won't leave you here alone."

"I won't *be* alone," said Lucy.

"Why not?"

"Because of Doris."

"Doris?"

"Yes, you know. My sister Doris. I phoned her, last

night, only the first time Pa answered, so I hung up, and then I called again and asked right off to speak to Doris. And then, tonight, when I said I needed the car and could you get a ride to work, I picked her up over in Berlin, from the bank where she's a teller, and brought her here. And everything's going to fix out just fine."

"Wait, Lucy, I don't understand," said Jake, sitting down across from her.

"Doris's going to come and stay with me, here in the apartment," Lucy said slowly. And then her words picked up speed, racing along like a train on a track. "Because she doesn't like being home with Pa, and she works in this bank over in Berlin and they're always looking for someone to work in the Ocean City branch, only nobody wants to in the wintertime. But mostly on account of she's my sister. And then I won't be alone, and she'll be here for the rest of the childbirth classes and be my birthing partner, only it won't be the same as you being here. And she even told me about the quilt."

"What quilt?" said Jake, shaking his head.

"The quilt Ma's making, with the Noah's Ark and all the animals, and how she used to work on it when she was home alone and then a couple of weeks ago how she brought it out one night and said, right in front of Pa, that she needed more time to work on it or else it wouldn't be done in time for her to take to her grandchild."

"Your mother said that?"

"Yes."

"And what'd your father say?" said Jake.

"Doris said as how Pa made out he didn't hear, on account of, that way, then he wouldn't have to say *anything*.

And now every night Ma sits there and sews and she's already done with the elephants and lions and now she's on the giraffes." Lucy reached across the table and put her hand on top of his. "Don't you see, Jake, how we have to take the chance to make sure forever that I didn't just latch on to you and you to me. Don't you see?"

Jake turned his hand so that their fingers interlocked and they sat there, together, at the kitchen table.

Thirteen

Jake is gone. I say it over to myself because if I hear it often enough then maybe I can get on with thinking about the rest: about how we spent Christmas at our place with Chrissie and T.J. and Jake's boss from up at the Pier. Captain Casey from the Beach Patrol was here, too, and the lady from the laundromat. Even Sid from Sid's Auto Repair, who worked on the Toyota once in exchange for Jake helping him to paint his house. In fact, near about the whole winter population of Ocean City seemed to be coming in and out of the apartment, some of them carrying cakes and casseroles and bowls of popcorn.

We'd thought about spending the day alone together, just the two of us, but we knew right off it'd be too sad.

We'd thought about ignoring it, but we couldn't, on

account of this was my first chance ever for a Christmas tree and to go to church at midnight on Christmas Eve, and besides, we liked walking along the boardwalk in the cold and the dark, singing carols at the top of our lungs.

We'd thought about going back to Smithfield, but we didn't, and George and Emma sent our presents here: a sweater for Jake and a nightgown with ruffles on it for me, and a stack of picture books for the baby all tucked into a set of bookends shaped like cats.

That's how come we ended up with this sort of day-long party, and the best thing about it was that Doris was here and she and Jake got to know each other better and he taught her how to help me with my breathing. For when I'm in labor, if he's not with me. And he probably won't be. Because of Baltimore being three and a half hours away and babies sometimes happening fast.

Jake is gone. He left this morning, and I drove him to the bus depot, because one thing Jake said right off was that I had to keep the car, to get to the doctor's and all, along with the stereo, his surfboard, his bike, and the pictures of Hector and Presilla. So's they'll be here when he gets back.

"But what if he doesn't. Get back, I mean." That thought kept poking at me, and after the bus'd pulled away, I drove up and parked by the boardwalk and got out, pulling my coat around me and tying my hood and walking, head bowed, into the wind. "Jake and I love each other," I called to the sea gulls and the clouds and the sand pushed up against the jetties. "Jake and I love each other." The thoughts kept at me, though, all about how maybe Jake'd meet somebody else and change his mind about us. Or I would. How, after being apart like this, things might never be the same again, for either one of us. Not in a hundred million years. And all the while the wind blew and the ocean roared, it was as if I had to think on these things— like turning on the light and staring down a noise in the dark.

I got to the end of the boardwalk and stood for a while, holding on to the rail and shaking from more than the cold, trying to catch my breath. My face burned and my fingers were numb inside my gloves. But when I turned around and started back, the wind was behind me and I fairly skimmed along, all the way to where I'd left the car. Afterwards I came to McDonald's for a milk shake and so's I could get properly warm. I've been sitting here by the window for near about an hour, thinking about Jake heading up the highway toward his dogsbody job with Adrian Blair, about me, and the baby, and all the things stretching out ahead for the three of us that we don't even know about yet. And how it's scary and exciting both at the same time.

I'm ready now, and I'll go and get Doris and she'll come home with me and we'll put my stuff in the bedroom, where the crib's already set up, and her stuff in the living room, and then maybe we'll go out and I'll show her the library and the laundromat and what the beach's like in wintertime.

I'll go now and this time I'll drive right up to the house, only Pa won't be there, 'cause Doris said he had to see a man over Salisbury way. But Ma'll be there and maybe she'll come out. Or maybe I'll get brave and go inside and see Warren and Liddy and where I used to live, and even that moldy old parrot.

And maybe I'll get to see the quilt. The one Ma's making for the baby.

And as far as the rest—everything else—it's going to be okay. One way or another, it's going to be okay.